FOR THE MEMORY OF DRAGONS

The Dragons of Eternity Series

JULIE WETZEL

For my favorite brother, Forest.
I love you. Call home!

FOR THE MEMORY OF DRAGONS
Copyright ©2015 Julie Wetzel
All rights reserved.
CTP Publishing, New York

SUMMARY: What do you do when a dragon crash-lands in your backyard? That's the question Terra's faced with when one of these creatures plows down into her cornfield. Should she help out the hunk of a man the dragon turns into, or turn him over to the trigger-happy 'authorities' that have come looking for him? The deciding factor—he has no memory. Now she must find out who he is.

ISBN: 978-1-63422-494-9 (paperback)
ISBN: 978-1-63422-146-7 (e-book)
COVER DESIGN BY: Marya Heidel
TYPOGRAPHY BY: Courtney Knight
EDITING BY: Cynthia Shepp

Prologue

Beating his wings hard, Alex pushed past the pain and raced higher into the sky. Droplets of water brushed over his face as he broke into the cloud cover. *Safe*.

Without a direct line of sight, the mage firing at him wouldn't be able to get a clean shot in. His muscles quivered from the two glancing blows he'd already taken while trying to escape. Swallowing back his grief, he clutched his leather bag against his chest. He had to get this information to Daniel before more dragons died at the hands of these monsters.

Pushing himself as fast as his injuries would let him, Alex pulled a sharp turn, hoping his attackers would follow the original course he'd set. He turned a few more times before letting his instincts take over and lead him off in the direction he needed to go.

The soft caress of the clouds lifted, and Alex found himself in open skies. The whip of the air lapped the moisture from his scales, cooling his heated skin. It felt wonderful. For all of ten seconds.

White-hot currents of electricity cracked across his hide, taking him by surprise. How the hell had that mage tracked him through the clouds? Alex tried to roar in pain, but everything had seized up as the bolt of magic raced through his body. He clenched his twitching muscles around his satchel as he spun out of control. No matter what happened, he couldn't lose that bag and its contents.

Forcing his unresponsive wings out, Alex tried to right himself, but he only managed to propel himself into an odd spin. He tried to gain his bearings so he could pull himself out of the fall, but his muscles refused to work properly. Everything was numb from the electrical shock. The only thing he was sure of was the ground was closing fast and this was going to hurt. A lot.

Chapter 1

An explosion rattled the windows of the old farmhouse, wrenching Terra from her book. She cursed as she fell off the couch and scrambled towards the windows at the back of the house. It was nice, living out in the middle of nowhere, but it meant that she had to be more aware of the things going on in the area around her.

Sure she would find a fireball that went with the explosion, Terra scanned the skyline. A cloud of dust rose from the cornfield just behind her house. Cursing again, she dropped her book on the floor. Something had to have come down over there, and someone could be hurt. She thought about grabbing her cell phone, but the reception out here was crap.

First aid kit! She grabbed the box from the kitchen and jammed her feet into her shoes. *Possible fire!* Nabbing the fire extinguisher from the stove, she raced out the back door.

Terra's thoughts turned to what could have fallen

from the sky as she pushed through the rows of corn. *A plane?* Surely there would have been a bigger explosion if some aircraft had come down. *A meteor?* That would be cool to see. Racing through the rows, her mind worked on the possibilities.

Completely distracted by the potential of the fallen object, Terra missed the huge groove the thing had cut in the crops as it dropped from the sky. Tripping on the edge, she tumbled down into the bottom of the furrow. Pulling herself up, she looked around for the wreckage. Oddly, there was none. No scraps of metal or chunks of anything that could have broken up upon impact.

Getting to her feet, Terra clutched her fire extinguisher. Just because there wasn't a fire to put out didn't mean that she didn't need it. Something had to have torn the great crater in the ground. If necessary, the heavy object would be great for bludgeoning whatever alien popped out of the corn.

Carefully, she made her way down the churned-up path. Seeing movement at the end, she raised her fire extinguisher, ready to swing it. The dirt exploded from the ground, and a mythical beast popped out.

Terra screamed and scrambled away as a dragon thrashed about, trying to stand up. It let out a weak roar and collapsed in a heap of wings and tail.

Terra peeked out from where she had taken refuge in the cornstalks.

The creature took a deep breath and snorted.

Of course, Terra knew dragons weren't really mythical creatures. Although she'd been very young at the time, she still remembered when the dragon king had paraded his entourage around, showing off the fact that dragons were, indeed, real. And there were plenty of dragons on TV, but to have a real-live dragon in her backyard was something else entirely.

Or dead. Terra eyed the great, blue beast as it lay in the dirt. It was unnervingly still.

Creeping closer, Terra reached out to touch the shimmering scales on the thing's shoulder. They were smooth and hard like polished glass or carefully chiseled bits of sapphire. She stroked the warm scales, awed by their iridescent quality. Logically, she knew this was an intelligent creature, but it looked so much like an animal, with those wickedly pointed horns and razor-sharp teeth, she wasn't sure what she should do.

The dragon let out a groan and shivered. Magic shimmered across the creature, reducing its massive bulk to the size of a man. He curled on his side in the dirt, naked as the day he was born.

Shock rooted Terra to the ground for a moment before she could shake it off. Now *this* she could handle. A man, even a naked man, was a whole lot better than that towering bulk of dragon.

"Hey."

She patted him gently on the shoulder, but he didn't move. Grabbing his shoulder, she pulled him onto his back. Reaching down, Terra checked his pulse, praying he was alive. A steady beat met her fingers. *Good. A live, naked man was much better than a dead, naked man any day of the week.*

"Hey fella."

She tried smacking him on the cheek lightly, but he

was out cold. *Great.* She glanced around at the cornfield. The weather was starting to turn a little chilly, and she couldn't leave him out here, exposed as he was. She looked back down at him. He was easily twice her size and stacked to hell and back. There was no way she was going to be able to get him up and out of the cornfield by herself.

Standing up, she dusted the dirt off her pants and tried to get her mind back in gear. For goodness' sake, she was a farm girl and had dealt with bigger issues than this. Running her eyes over the fallen man, she couldn't help but notice other things about him that she would consider a big issue.

Jerking her eyes back under control, she grabbed up her safety kit and fire extinguisher and headed back to the farmhouse. She dumped her supplies off in the kitchen and went to the living room. A blanket—that's what she really needed. Ignoring the small afghan on the couch, she decided to go with the much larger quilt from her bed. So what if she got the handmade bedding a little dirty? When someone dropped that much beefcake in your backyard, you needed something extra large to cover it.

Stopping on the porch, an idea hit Terra. She may not be able to lift him by herself, but she could probably roll him into something and drag his ass back to the house. Heading into the barn, she spied an old wheelbarrow. *Perfect!* She flipped it over and dumped her bedding in the cart. Now all she needed to do was get him in it. No problem.

Problem. The man was a whole lot denser then Terra

ever dreamed possible. That much limp bulk was proving to be a pain in her backside.

"Come *on*!"

She groaned as she yanked on him, trying to get him up and into the bed of the cart. Giving up on the idea of lifting him, Terra draped the blanket over the man's body and laid the wheelbarrow on its side.

"Get *in* there."

Grunting, she shoved him backwards into the cart. Pushing on the top side, she managed to get the wheelbarrow upright, but it scooped both of them up together.

"Damn it!" she cursed as she flailed around, trying to get free. This was just what she needed—to be stuck in a wheelbarrow with a naked man.

Finally, she managed to get untangled from the guy and out of the cart without tipping it over again. "God, you're heavy," Terra complained as she sat on the ground, resting.

After a few minutes, she stood up and flipped the blanket back over the unconscious man. It was a shame not to appreciate something so fine, but she needed to concentrate if she had any hope of getting him back to the house. Glancing around the crater, she found something that didn't belong. A leather bag. Grabbing it up, she tossed it in the wheelbarrow with her load and worked on getting the whole mess back to the house.

STOPPING at the bottom of the steps, Terra looked up at the porch. *Problem number two.* How in the hell was she supposed to get this dumb lug onto the porch? She couldn't pull the cart close and drag him out—the railing was in the way. And she couldn't push or pull the wheelbarrow up the steps—they were much too steep.

Pondering this for a moment, she pushed the cart next to the bottom step. Sure enough, if she worked the wheelbarrow up onto the bottom step, the front edge of the bed would almost touch the porch. If she could get it up there, she should be able to just slide him out.

Shoving with everything she had, Terra managed to get the lip of the bed up onto the edge of the porch, she pushed the handles up, expecting him to slide out. A resounding thud sounded from the other side of the bed, and she dropped the empty cart to find her mystery man hadn't slid out at all; he'd fallen out. Right on his face.

"Oh shit!" She pushed the wheelbarrow out of the way and went to see if he was hurt. "I'm so glad you're unconscious right now, buddy."

Pulling him over, Terra grimaced at the huge, red spot forming on his forehead. *Ouch!* He was definitely going to feel that one later. She touched it gently, feeling the nice goose egg that had already formed.

"Sorry," she whispered as she pulled him straight again.

Taking the blanket, she shook the dirt from it and laid the clean bedding down next to him. Grabbing a broom, she dusted the soil off the man. Once he was clean, she rolled him onto the blanket, flipped the end over him again, and tossed his bag on top of the pile.

Glancing over her handiwork, she smiled. *Good.* It wouldn't have been very pleasant if she had left him tucked in the blanket with all that dirt.

Terra grabbed the end of the blanket and dragged him inside. His head only bounced a little as she manhandled him over the threshold.

"Come on." She gritted her teeth as she pulled his heavy bulk inside.

Stopping for a breather, Terra stretched the muscles in her back. She was going to need a long soak in a hot bath after this workout. Getting back to dragging him inside, she ignored the strained muscles in her back and concentrated on all the calories she was burning instead.

A fire crackled in the fireplace as Terra shoved the rug out of the way and dropped her burden in front of the hearth. A freak storm had passed through the area yesterday and dropped several trees, downing power and phone lines. The utility companies were hard at work fixing the issues, but the power was still out. Thankfully, she had a working fireplace to cut the chill in the air. Terra dropped a new log on the fire before turning to her unconscious guest.

Picking up the leather bag, she tossed it onto the couch, out of the way. She'd get to that later. Right now, she had something more interesting to investigate. Flipping the blanket back, Terra checked the dragon man for injuries.

"Man, you're *fine*," she said as studied him.

In addition to having well-toned muscles, his skin was a beautiful bronze that came from either sunbathing or working outdoors naked. *How the hell didn't he have tan lines?*

Lifting his arm, she checked to make sure each joint bent how it was supposed to, and that the bones didn't bend at all. She also looked for suspicious bruising. There wasn't any. There was, however, a very interesting tattoo of a figure eight on the back of his shoulder. Terra traced it and tried to figure out why someone would draw a line down the middle of an eight. *Weird.* Giving up, she laid him back down and pulled the blanket back around him.

Running her fingers through his messy, blond hair, she pushed it back, looking for other wounds. The only thing she found was the lump where his forehead had met with her porch. Pretty sure he would survive, Terra sat back and studied her guest.

"Now what?" she asked out loud, but he didn't answer.

Of course he wouldn't answer—the man was dead to the world. Letting out a long sigh, she stood up. She probably should get something for the lump on his head before he woke up.

"Hang on, I'll be right back," she said and went into the kitchen to see what she could round up.

Terra thought about calling the police, but the authorities were busy with cleanup from the storm that had passed through the area. The last thing they needed was to have to make a trip way out here. She decided against calling for help. Since the man wasn't broken or bleeding, he probably didn't need an emergency crew, and that's what the police would send. Maybe he wouldn't be out very long. And if he were, she could always call for help later.

Grabbing a mostly frozen bag of peas and cubed carrots from the freezer, Terra smacked it on the counter to break it up. With the power out, she didn't want to use what little ice she had. It was probably the only thing keeping her fridge cold. Plus, she could use the veggies in dinner later. Grabbing a dishtowel, she wrapped the bag up and went back to the living room.

The man hadn't moved, so she rested the cold pack on the lump. Spying one of the throw pillows on the couch, Terra snagged it and slipped it under the man's head. He didn't need a crick in his neck to go with the headache she was sure he was going to have.

Terra sat on the couch and watched him sleep for a while. He looked so peaceful. She had never had a gorgeous guy stretched out in front of her fire, all naked and vulnerable. *Oh, the possibilities.* She shook her head to drive that thought out. Her mind had taken a turn for the creepy, and that just wasn't her.

Instead, she turned her attention to the bag next to her. Maybe there was something in it that would tell her who he was. The outside of the bag was pretty plain except for a symbol worked into the flap. Terra ran her finger over the sideways eight with a line running across it. It was the same as on the man's shoulder.

Laughing, she shook her head at her own stupidity. *It wasn't an eight. It was an infinity symbol! But why would someone draw a line through it?* It kind of looked familiar, but she couldn't place where she'd seen it before. Shrugging, she flipped the flap open and looked inside. The contents were disappointing.

The bag was nearly empty. It held a single file with a stack of papers in it and a silver necklace. Reaching in, Terra pulled out the necklace. It wasn't exceptionally pretty, but it did have some neat scrollwork to the round charm. It tingled against her fingers, like it had a low current running through it. Terra didn't know much about magic, but this piece was definitely magical. Dropping it back in the bag, she pulled out the file. Things suddenly became a whole lot more interesting. There was a big stamp across the front that read *Classified*.

Flipping the file open, Terra found a picture of a beautiful woman pinned to the top of what looked like one of those police identification pages they used for suspects. Terra read over the page. The description of the girl was just as fascinating as her picture. Terra gasped and glanced back up at the picture when she reached the woman's birth date. She didn't look more than thirty, but the listed age was over three hundred years old! *Holy freaking cow!* A box further down the page labeled the woman as a red dragon.

How freaking old do dragons get! Terra glanced up at the man stretched out on her floor. *And if he looks to be in his mid-twenties, how old is he?*

Turning back to the file, she read on. At the bottom of the page, there was a handwritten note. It was an eyewitness account of the woman's last sighting. Apparently, she had gone missing within the last month and was presumed dead.

Terra turned to the next page. This one had a picture of a smiling man—another dragon—and again, it listed him as missing, presumed dead, with an account of his last sighting. Terra flipped through the twenty or so pages. Each was a description of a dragon that had gone missing. None of the pictures matched the man on her floor. Folding the file back together, she returned it to the pouch. Searching the rest of the bag revealed a bunch of nothing: a few dollars, a book of matches, and some gum. *Boy, this guy wasn't making life easy.*

Dropping the bag back to the floor, she shoved it under the couch and got up. Her stomach was telling her it was time for food. Terra pulled the melted vegetables off the dragon man's face and checked on the lump. It was starting to look pretty good. Still a little red, but the swelling had gone down. Given a little more time, the mark would be gone, and she wouldn't have to explain how she had dropped him on his face.

She considered him for a minute. With that file full of missing persons, he could be some kind of cop or a private detective. But didn't they have to keep a badge or something? And what had made him crash in her cornfield? Tossing the bag of vegetables in the air as she walked, she went into the kitchen to start dinner. Maybe he would be awake by the time it was ready, and she could ask him.

Chapter 2

What the hell! Terra cursed to herself as she dropped her spoon in the pot and headed out of the kitchen. She was going to beat whoever was banging on her front door like that. She paused to check on her sleeping dragon. He was still breathing. *Good.* Heading over to the door, she yanked it open. The sight that met her stopped her before she could start yelling. *Shit.*

"Where the hell have you been, woman?"

Derrick, her ex-boyfriend, stood on the porch with two bags in his arms.

"Open this goddamn door and let me in."

"Derrick!" She gasped. "What are you doing here?"

What in the hell could this asshole want now?

Having left her three months ago, Terra had never expected to see Derrick back at her door. He had dumped her faster than a knife fight in a phone booth when the hot chick he'd been chasing had finally given in. It had torn her up at first, but a little reflecting on their relationship had changed her mind. In retrospect, he hadn't been the nice guy she had taken him for.

Derrick tugged on the locked screen door. "A tree fell on the shop. Now open the door."

Clutching the inside door, Terra looked at the horror revisiting her. At first, Derrick had been a great guy—loving and sweet. But, man, once he'd moved in, he had turned over a few new leaves. Suddenly, nothing she did was right, and oh, the temper tantrums he threw! It took her a while to realize that the problem wasn't her. And thankfully, he'd left before things had gotten physical. She would put up with a lot of things in the name of love, but abuse was not one of them.

Terra pulled her shoulders straight and glared at him. "What happened to your girlfriend?"

"That bitch didn't deserve me. Open this damn door." He rattled the screen door again.

Apparently, this shithead doesn't realize he's out of luck.

"No," Terra answered and went to slam the door in his face.

"Damn it, bitch!" Derrick jerked the screen door hard enough to crack the frame. "If you shut that door, so help me, I will kill you." He tugged on the loosening door again.

Terra was sure Derrick had meant every word he'd said, but she didn't care. She wasn't going to let some abusive shit back into her life.

"Leave before I call the cops."

She tried to shut the door, but it wouldn't move. An arm wrapped around her shoulders, drawing her back into a very warm body.

"The lady told you to leave," a deep voice rumbled from behind her.

Whoa! Terra glanced back to see the dragon man holding her against him. *When the hell had he woken up?*

Derrick stopped tugging on the door and glared at the man. "Who the hell are you, and what are you doing with my woman?"

"I'm the one that's going to beat the hell out of you if you touch her, and I don't think she's your woman anymore. Leave. Now."

With that, the dragon man pulled the door from Terra's hand and slammed it in Derrick's face.

Nice!

Derrick's scream of outrage echoed through the door, but he stomped his way down the steps and out of her life again. Apparently, he felt at ease threatening a woman but wouldn't stand up to a man.

Good riddance! Hopefully, he will stay gone this time. Now she just had to deal with the naked man holding on to her. *This was going to be... interesting.*

ALEX DROPPED his head to the young woman's shoulder as his world spun. He really shouldn't have gotten up from the floor, but listening to someone threatening the girl had pissed him off.

"I didn't mean to intrude on your personal business," he apologized.

"Much appreciated," the young woman answered. They stood there together for a long moment with him leaning on her shoulder. "Umm… You can let me go now."

"Ha!" Alex let out a mirthless laugh and shook his head. "I would, but you're the only thing keeping me on my feet right now." If he loosened his hold on her, he was going to fall over.

She turned in his grip and wrapped her arms around him, taking his weight. "God, I'm sorry."

"It's all right." He leaned on her as she led him across the room to the couch.

"I'm Terra, by the way," she said, introducing herself as they walked. "What's your name?"

Alex opened his mouth to answer, but his brain flat-lined. He couldn't recall his own name! In fact, he had no idea where he was or why he was naked. He stopped, waiting for the answer to come to him, but nothing did.

"At the moment, I have no idea," Alex admitted. His head was pounding. Maybe he'd hit it or something.

Terra looked at him, concerned. "It will come back to you," she offered.

He let her pull him back into motion.

"You took a nasty fall."

Well, that might explain why he felt like a truck had hit him, backed up to see what they'd hit, and then run over him again. God, he hurt. He looked down, expecting to see bruises and blood everywhere, but there wasn't any. Just him, naked.

"What happened to my clothing?" Alex asked as she helped him to the couch and handed him the afghan from the back. He tucked it around his waist.

"You weren't wearing any when I found you," Terra

said. She picked up the blanket from the floor, folded it, and laid it over his legs. It was bigger than the afghan and covered him all the way to the floor. "In fact, you weren't even human when I found you," she added casually.

Okay, well that explained why he didn't have clothing. He must have been in dragon form. *Oh that's nice!* He remembered he was a dragon, but he still had no clue what his name was. The little voice in the back of his head that he recognized as his dragon part snickered at him. He felt the bright flash of scales slither across the back of his mind, reminding him that he had something important to do, but the pain in his head kept him from coming up with what. Lifting a hand, Alex pressed his fingers into his temple, trying to get the pounding to subside.

"I don't want to impose on you further, but do you have anything for pain? I think I might have hit my head."

"Sure," Terra answered.

Is that amusement *in her voice, or something else? Does she know something I don't?* Before he could work out what to say, she called to him from the kitchen.

"Anything in particular?"

He didn't care what she gave him, just as long as it made his head stop pounding. Alex shook his head no and instantly regretted it. He leaned it on the back of the couch, hoping the extra support would help. It felt like someone had tried to get into it with a sledgehammer.

"Here." Terra held out her hand towards him.

Alex sat back up and took what she offered. "Thank you." He looked at the two mismatched pills and the can of coke. *What in the world?*

He glanced up at her, confused.

"Aspirin, acetaminophen, and caffeine," Terra explained. "The two meds work differently, and the caffeine will help them along. The sugar in there might do you some good, too."

Whatever. As long as they worked.

Popping the pills in his mouth, he washed them down with the coke, then pressed the cold can to the sore spot on his forehead. *God, that felt good!* Closing his eyes, he listened as Terra found a seat on the loveseat next to the couch.

"So, how do you feel?"

That's a stupid question. He'd just told her that his head ached.

"I hurt."

He took one more drink of the coke before resting it on the couch and leaning his head back again.

"I don't doubt it a bit," Terra said. "You did manage to dig a massive furrow in the cornfield."

Rolling his head over, Alex cracked an eye to look at her. She was smiling at him, but it wasn't an amused smile. It was more sympathetic.

"You were either moving fast or came down hard."

He closed his eye and rolled his head back into its place. "Both, if I had to guess by the way I feel."

Oh yes, hard and fast. What in the hell could take a dragon out of the sky? A quick flash of memory skimmed through his mind—blue sky and a flash of light. *Had there been a*

19

lighting strike? That could potentially drop a dragon. He tried to get the memory to come back, but it just made his head hurt worse. *Great.*

"Is there anything I can do for you? Someone I should call?"

Bells and whistles went off in his brain as his dragon growled. There was something he was forgetting. Well, he couldn't remember a lot of things, but there was something really, really important that he needed to remember. And it had to do with contacting—or not contacting—someone.

Unable to figure it out, he shook his head slightly. "No. I just need to rest for a bit."

Yes, a nice nap should help greatly! Leaning his head over on the couch, he let go. The tingle of magic raced across his body as his dragon half took over. A few hours in his lesser form should go a long way to making him feel better. And maybe being closer to his instincts would let him remember the things he'd forgotten. Like his name.

TERRA GASPED as a shimmer of magic swept across the man's body, reducing him to a miniature dragon. She had seen him shift from his large size to human, but she didn't know he could shift to a smaller size. *Amazing!*

The small dragon wiggled around on the couch until his head was tucked into the corner under the pillows. He pulled his wings in alongside his body and relaxed.

Terra studied him for a moment, fascinated. *He's adorable in this form.* With a body the size of a small

Labrador, she could almost imagine him as a dog. But his neck and tail were both much longer. Small versions of the back-sloping horns he'd had in the large size poked out from under the pillows, and his tail curled down to the floor. His scales were the same amazing blue. Standing up from her seat, Terra picked up the blanket and spread it over him.

"Rest as long as you need to." She patted him on the back.

He snorted into the pillow and let out a sound that was something like a purr.

Oh, how cute! Smiling, Terra picked up his can of pop and took it back into the kitchen. Last thing she needed was for him to knock it over accidentally, and it wasn't like he would be able to pick it up and drink it in this form. Maybe she should pour it in a bowl for him? *Nah.* She placed the open can in the fridge and went back to the stove. Hopefully, she hadn't burnt dinner too badly.

Chapter 3

Another pounding on the front door pulled Terra away from the kitchen. *If that asshole is back, he is going to get what for!*

She grabbed her baseball bat from the broom cabinet before heading out. The weight felt good in her hands. Glancing at the couch, she found that her dragon man had moved and was now curled up completely under the blanket. Just a large lump under the comforter. *So cute.*

Turning her mind back to the knocking, she jerked open the door, ready to knock someone's head in. Two men dressed in suits stood on her porch.

"Hello," she said, dropping the bat down to her side. Their suits told her they were here on some kind of business. They didn't look like cops.

Maybe they're Mormons.

One of the men glanced at the bat before looking back at her face. "Good evening. Sorry for disturbing you. I'm Parker, and this is my partner, Brett. We're here with the FBI." He flashed some kind of badge but didn't leave it out long enough for Terra to read it.

Terra eyed the man. His white shirt shone brightly next to his dark skin. He seemed the FBI type, but his partner… well, that was another question altogether. The man's suit was nice, but he needed a shave. Badly. He was rather pale, and his short, brown hair stuck out in odd angles.

"FBI?" Something didn't sit right with her.

"Yes, ma'am," Parker answered. He tugged on his jacket like that could make him more presentable. "We're looking for a suspect and wanted to know if you've seen anything strange today." He glanced down at the bat again.

"A suspect?" she asked. These two didn't have the right feel for FBI. Hit men, maybe.

"A dragon, to be precise," Parker clarified. "Have you seen anything like that today?"

A shiver raced through Terra, warning her of danger. These men were looking for the dragon on her couch. But turning him over didn't seem right.

"Well, to be honest, there have been several strange men in the area today."

The men perked up as if they had hit the jackpot. "Did you see someone? Can you tell me where they went?"

These men were way too excited about finding the dragon. Making a snap decision, Terra nodded.

"Oh yes! Something came down in the cornfield out behind my house." She batted her eyes at them and tried to play the innocent girl. "But I was too scared to go out and look."

"Can you show us?" Parker asked.

"Oh no. I didn't go out there. But if you want to go have a look, it was straight out behind the house." Terra laid the sweet-and-innocent routine on a little thick, hoping they would believe she was the helpless girl she was pretending to be. It all depended on how soft-hearted they were. Terra didn't think it would work for long, but it might get them to go out and check the back field. Sure, they would find the hole. With the darkness growing, they would probably fall in the sucker—hopefully breaking something.

Parker turned to Brett. "Go look."

Brett gave Parker a funny look and nodded. "Right."

Terra did not like the sarcastic way Brett drew out that word.

"Is it possible to come in and look around?" Parker asked. "I just want to make sure you're safe."

More warnings screamed in Terra's head. These men were up to no good. It was time to get her dragon and get the hell out of there.

She smiled at them warmly. "That's so nice of you. Give me a moment to put Cookie in his kennel. He doesn't like visitors."

"Cookie?" Parker asked.

"My dog." Terra grinned and shut the door on the man.

Shit! Shit! Shit!

Grabbing her purse, she slung the thing over her shoulder. She needed to get out of there fast. Pulling the satchel out from under the couch, she slipped that on, too. It might be important to her dragon. She figured Parker would give her about two minutes before he started knocking again. Now came the hard part.

Wrapping her arms around the dragon, she scooped him up, blanket and all. He let out a squeak as she disturbed him, thrashing about in her hold.

"Settle down, Cookie." She spoke in a loud voice. "You don't want to scare the visitors."

The blanket froze.

"Good boy."

She glanced back at the windows next to the door. Her momma had always taught her to keep those curtains drawn, but with the fading light outside, there was a chance Parker might be able to seen in. The lump in the blanket softened. *Great!* Now she could carry him without him fighting. Apparently, dragons did understand human speech. She had been worried for a moment.

"That's a good boy!" She ruffled the bundle in case the man was watching.

The bundle growled at her.

She smiled at the rumbling mass. Popping the bundle on the bottom, she gathered up the blanket and wrapped it around him more. "That's no way to behave, Cookie."

Now, it was time to get out of here. Walking to the kitchen, she heard Brett on the back porch. *Checking the cornfield, indeed!* Thankfully, she had locked the door. She flicked off the stove as she passed. It wouldn't do to escape and then let her house burn down.

"Come on, Cookie, let's get you settled." She opened the door to the cellar. "In you get."

Walking in, she closed the door behind her. The men wouldn't wait much longer before breaking in. She snapped the deadbolt into place with her key. The only way they would get through that was either with the key —one of twenty in her junk drawer—or by breaking the door in. And that was a pretty stout door.

Hurrying down the steps, she moved by memory through the dark. *Thirteen steps down. Boxes at the bottom. Right. Ten paces to the wall. Left.* The sound of her back door being forced open drove her steps faster. *Fifteen paces to the storm shelter.* She caught the bottom of the shelf built into the door with her foot and swung the thing open. Slipping into the dark corridor just as the men started beating on the basement door, Terra pulled the door back into place behind her. It was damn dark in there and hard to tell if the shelf was seated right, but by the time the men got the door open and found her exit, she would be long gone.

Now came the fun part—making her way down the less-familiar corridor. She used to play down here as a kid, but that had been a long time ago.

The bundle in her arms wiggled.

"Be still," she whispered to the dragon.

He immediately stopped moving.

Hurrying down the path by memory, she stumbled on the bottom step of the exit stairs. *Shit.* The path wasn't as long as she remembered it being. Cuddling the dragon to her, she raced up the steps and stopped at the wooden hatch covering her exit.

"Just stay still," she warned the dragon.

It rumbled in response.

Taking that as an "okay," Terra set him on the top step and carefully released the latch. She pushed the hatch up and stopped when the rusty hinge started to squeak loudly. She peeked out through the narrow slit, praying the noise hadn't drawn the men's attention. Both of the men were in her kitchen, ramming their shoulders into her basement door. *Suckers!*

Grabbing the dragon back up, she shoved her shoulder into the trap door. It screeched open with a sound like a tortured cat and fell to the floor with a loud bang. The racket would definitely draw their attention, giving her mere seconds to get to her car before the men saw her. But it was better than being caught. Sprinting to the driveway, she yanked open the driver's door and tossed the blanket-wrapped dragon inside the car. She threw herself into the driver's seat behind him.

Yelling came from her back porch as she jammed the key into the slot and fired the car up. A gunshot sounded as she threw it into gear.

Holy shit! These guys aren't messing about. Who the hell is this dragon?

Slamming the gas pedal to the floor, she tore off through the grass towards the road. She didn't have time to spare a glance at the bundle of dragon as she dodged around trees and aimed for the ditch. Peeking up into her mirror, she saw that the men had jumped into their SUV and were gaining on her. *Perfect!*

Terra squeezed through the gap in the trees and over the ditch with the precision of a brain surgeon. Yanking the wheel to the right, she tuned sharply. The tires grabbed the pavement and slung them into a new direction. The bundle of dragon slid across the seat into her hip. It chirped loudly in protest. *Poor dragon.* She patted it before looking back up at the mirror. The SUV was just getting to the crossing. Her heart skipped when the SUV bounded oddly across the gap. *Yes!*

The guys made the turn, and both of the left-side tires blew from where the metal edging of the culvert had cut into them. Terra danced in her seat. There were many times she'd hit that pipe wrong and cut a tire. And making that sharp turn onto the blacktop—perfect recipe for disaster! Too bad they didn't roll the car when the tires blew.

Now all she had to do was find an out-of-the-way spot to lie low; maybe then she could get some answers from her mystery man. She knew just the place, and there were farm tools to use for torture if need be. *Oh yeah!*

DAMN IT, *woman!*

Alex wiggled around in the comforter, trying to find a way out. That crazy woman had snatched him up, wrapped him in a blanket, and now expected him to be still. And where did she come off calling him Cookie? Now they were God knows where, doing God knows what, at God knows what speed. When he got out of this blanket, he was going to give her a piece of his mind!

Light leaked in around the edges of his prison, and he poked his head towards it. *Finally! Air!*

"Crazy woman!" he chirped in dragon.

She reached her hand down and patted his back. "It's okay, Cookie."

Cookie!

"My name is not *Cookie!*" he snarled at her.

She looked down at him, shocked. "Someone woke up grumpy."

"Of course I'm grumpy. You would be, too, if someone wrapped you in a blanket and tossed you around." He growled and chirped complaints at her.

Struggling, he finally extracted himself from the blanket. *That thing was hot!* He kicked it to the floor, disgusted.

She let out a loud huff. "See if I save your ass again. I could have let those men have you."

Alex stopped and looked at her. "Men?" he chirped. "What men?" When Terra didn't answer him, he put his front foot on her leg. "What men?" He pushed down, trying to get her to answer.

"Hey!" Terra yanked his foot off her leg. "Those things are sharp."

"*What men?*" His wings ruffled in agitation. *Damn it, this was important.*

Terra glanced at him before turning her attention back to the road.

"*What men!*" he barked. *Can't this woman answer a simple question?*

She glared at him. "Go ahead and keep yelling at me." She turned her attention back to the road. "It won't do you any good. I don't understand 'squeak squeak squeakity squeak'."

Aarrrgggg! Of all the crazy, irritating women!

He paced in the car, aggravated. Couldn't she see this was important? If she wanted yelling, he would give her yelling! Closing his eyes, he turned his mind towards human and let go. Nothing happened. Frustrated, he took a deep breath and tried again. Still, he remained a dragon.

Crap! Of all the times to get stuck in dragon form, why now?

He circled on the seat, irritated. A hand came down on his back, knocking him off balance.

"Sit!" Terra barked and forced him down on the seat. "You're going to make me wreck."

Growling, he settled on the seat. *Fine!* He would sit. He wiggled around, stretching out on the seat. It was really too small for him, so he squirmed closer to her and laid his head in her lap. *Oh, yes.* That gave him the space he needed.

Closing his eyes, he turned his mind to the problem at hand. Why couldn't he shift? Memories filtered in. Other times he had gotten stuck in dragon form, so this problem wasn't anything new. He worked on those memories and came up with an answer he could use— his dragon half had gotten stubborn and taken over. He wasn't listening to it properly, or he was missing something important. Yeah, he was missing something important right now—his memory! *Fine.* If his dragon wanted to speak, he would listen.

Drawing in a deep breath, Alex relaxed. First, he had to deal with the irritation. A few quick breathing exercises calmed his heart and eased the anger away. Relaxing more, he let go of all thought and reveled in being a dragon. His senses sharpened, and he took note of the things around him. The gentle rocking of the car. The hum of road noise. The rub of the steering wheel against one of his horns. He rolled his head away from the wheel so Terra could drive without that interference. The movement pressed his head into her body. She was warm and soft. And smelled nice. Like woman and flowers.

He slowly became aware of soft fingers gliding back and forth over his scales. She was petting him. Usually that irritated him, but this felt nice. His dragon was content with her touch. Now that was odd—usually his dragon was cranky. He stopped and thought about that. *So his dragon* did *remember.* Turning to that piece of him, he asked the question he needed to know. *Who am I?*

A torrent of memories flooded him, all from the viewpoint of a dragon. The feel of air over scales. The taste of smoke and flame. The sting of another dragon's claws as they were wrapped together in passion. He lingered on that memory for a moment and was able to remember the girl. She was a passing fancy that his dragon had tolerated. Going on, more images flooded his brain. Training. Lots and lots of training. The bite of claws. The sting of flames. His buddies congratulating him when he made his goal. He had earned the right to wear that tattoo on his shoulder. The one human memory he recalled was the sting of the needle as it embedded the ink into his skin. Everything came to him in flashes of sensation, but no sound. It gave him a sense of what he was—he was an Elite—but he still had no idea *who* he was.

The soft scratching of Terra's nails over his scales stopped as she turned the car in somewhere and shut it off. They had arrived at wherever they were going.

Good. It was high time they both got some answers.

Chapter 4

afe. Terra turned off the car and looked down at the dragon in her lap. At least he wasn't growling and chirping at her anymore. *Damn, was he grumpy.* She rested her hand back down on him. He was also warm and smooth. Something she could really get used to. Terra shook her head, driving the silly thought out. He may look like a pet, but he was really a man. Something she should remember.

She patted him gently on the shoulder. "Wake up."

The dragon cracked his eye and looked up at her.

Wow! His eyes were gorgeous.

"I think it's time we talked." Terra patted him again.

He lifted his head up and chirped at her.

Terra just shook her head. "We're going to have to work on your communication skills, buddy."

The dragon snickered and nodded his head.

"Can you change back?" Terra looked at him, calculating how big he would be in human form. He might fit, lying in the seat like that. It would be entertaining to see him try. A chirp interrupted her musing.

Turning around, the dragon caught hold of the door with his teeth and tried to pull it open. *So cute!*

"Here." Terra leaned over him and yanked on the handle. The door popped open.

The dragon gave her another chirp and hopped out onto the floor of the barn.

Grabbing her door, she pushed it open and looked around the barn. This was the perfect place to talk with him. A twinkling of glass shone in the corner—the only evidence that this barn had surveillance in it.

"I'm sorry I snapped at you."

Terra turned around and saw that her dragon had turned back into a man. "As well you should be." She slammed the door and started around the car. "I just saved your ass back there, buddy. You should be at least a little grateful."

She stopped as soon as she got around the front of the car. He was standing there, buck naked. Again.

"Don't you have any sense of decency?" She stormed over and pushed past him. "Geez." Pulling her quilt out of the car, she thrust it at him. "Cover that thing up. A girl can only take so much." Turning her head away from him, she tried to find something interesting to look at on the floor.

Snickering, he reached for the blanket. One hand took the blanket, while the other caught Terra's wrist.

Terra's eyes shot up to meet his.

"Thank you."

The warmth in his voice sent a shiver down her

spine. The blanket slipped from her fingers as he dropped it and reached up to cup her cheek.

"For everything."

What was that? Terra glance away as heat crawled up her skin. "You're welcome." It was unnerving how his voice made her insides flutter. Pulling away from him, she shut the car door.

Snickering again, he picked up the blanket and wrapped it around his shoulders so it hung down around him. "Is this better?"

Terra glanced back. "Yes." It was almost a shame to have him cover up, but she really needed to talk to him without the distraction. She turned around and leaned on the side of the car. "I should let you know that this barn belongs to a friend of the family. He's a bit of a conspiracy nut, so we're under surveillance."

The dragon man nodded.

"So," Terra eyed him, "who are you?"

He let out a long sigh and turned to lean against the car beside her. "I don't know." He shook his head slowly.

Great. He still doesn't remember.

"Why were those men after you?"

Again, he shook his head slowly. His shoulders dropped into a depressed slouch.

"Then can you tell me what you know about this?" Terra pulled the file out of his bag and handed it to him.

The man took it and looked at it. Shock hit his face. *Oh, this triggered some memories!*

I KNOW THIS WOMAN!

The thought echoed around Alex's brain as he stared at the first profile in the folder. His knees weakened as he slid down the side of the car and sat on the floor, reading the file. He had memories of visits to her. He would bring her flowers; she would serve him tea. Everything was bright and sharp, but there was no sound. *Why don't any of my memories have sound?*

Flipping the page, he saw another person he knew. A man. This one collected models of classic cars. The next page contained another person he knew. All of the pages held faces of people he knew.

"I know these people." Alex said softly as he flipped back to the first page and reread what was there. The account of the woman's last sighting made his heart hurt. "I wrote this." He pointed to the paragraph at the bottom.

"So who are they?" Terra asked as she looked down at him.

"Friends," he answered.

No, that wasn't right.

"People I visited."

That was better. They were friends, but he did something for them more than just as a friend. *But what?* Now that was the question. Alex looked over the file again. All of the people were listed as missing, presumed dead. Each had an account of their last-known sighting. All but one.

Something important ate at the corner of his mind, but the more he chased after the thought, the more skittish it became. Giving up for now, he looked at the pages one more time before closing the file. The pages triggered some memories, but not the ones he needed.

"I don't know," he admitted and handed the folder back to Terra.

"Then what about this?" She shifted the bag to show him the symbol on the flap. "You have the same mark on your shoulder."

He raised his hand and rubbed his fingers over the mark. "It's special." He knew he had earned the right to wear it, but he couldn't remember what it stood for. "I don't know," he admitted again.

"There are other things in the bag." She pulled it off and handed it down to him. "I'm sorry, but I looked through it while you were sleeping."

Alex nodded and took the satchel. Crossing his legs, he leaned forwards and dumped the stuff out. *Damn.* There was nothing in there. He shifted through the trash, trying to make sense of it. Gum, matches, a necklace, and a few crumpled dollars. Nothing to help him remember.

The sting of magic bit his fingers when he picked up the necklace. "Shit," he cursed and dropped the thing. "What the hell is that?" Picking up the pack of gum, he used it to poke at the charm. It felt… evil.

Terra squatted next to him and picked up the necklace. "Some sort of charm."

He stared at her, surprised. That thing had stung him when he'd touched it. *How can she hold it like that?*

"That doesn't hurt?" he asked, bewildered.

Terra looked at the charm. "No." She flipped it over

to look at the back. "It tingles a little, but it doesn't hurt." She held it out to him.

"Uh uh." Alex held out the bag so Terra could drop the necklace in. "I ain't touching that thing again."

She gave him an odd look. "It *is* yours, right?"

"I guess so." He looked at the charm. "This is my bag, right?" The bag had a familiar feel to it, but he had no way to be sure.

"I found it with you, so it must be." She dropped the necklace into the bottom of the bag.

Alex looked at the small piece of silver. "Then it must be mine." He took the file from her and tucked it back in the bag, too. Next, he looked at the gum and box of matches. They were both unopened. He dropped the gum in the bag. The box of matches intrigued him. It had the name of a pub on it—The Dragon's Flight. "Do you know this place?" He held the box out for Terra to see.

"No." Terra took the matches and flipped them over. "But there's an address on them. I'm sure we could find it."

"We should probably start there." Alex held his hand out for the box.

She gave it back.

"Maybe someone there will know who I am."

A small laugh came out of Terra. She rested her hand on his shoulder reassuringly. "We will find out who you are," she promised, "but we should probably start with finding you clothing. I don't think they would like you in that pub wrapped in just a blanket."

"Point." Alex smiled up at her. "Clothing first. Then

food. Then we will go hunting." He didn't know about Terra, but his stomach was telling him he had missed more than one meal.

"Deal." Terra pressed down on his shoulder as she stood up.

He let out a soft sigh. The feel of her hand on him stirred things inside him. When she offered to help him up, he took it. Her hand was soft and warm in his. Desire washed through him, and it was all he could do not to pull her in against him. To feel her pressed into his body. His arms twitched with the impulse, but he stopped them before they could act. Alex knew where these feelings came from and understood the forces that drove dragons, but she was human. She would not understand mating instincts. Nor would she understand how his dragon side had latched onto her.

He pulled away from her and reached for the car. "So, where to first?" he asked. Maybe if he put some space between them, his instincts would settle down. Then again, maybe not.

WHAT JUST HAPPENED? Terra looked at her dragon man, confused. She had gotten the oddest feeling when he had taken her hand. The way he touched it. The look in his eye. Desire had shot through her. But then he had turned, and it was gone. Shaking herself, she answered his question. "Meijers."

He nodded as he climbed in the car.

Terra watched him as he sat in his seat with his head

down and eyes closed. There was something about him that drew her. Sure, she had always been a sucker for hard-luck cases, but still, most never sparked the feelings he did.

Circling around the car, she got in and started it up. It was weird with him in the car as a human. "So, what do you remember?" she asked, prodding him into talking before the silence could get stifling. There was something going on that she didn't understand.

Her dragon man let out a deep sigh. "Not much." His brow furrowed as he thought. "Just pieces."

"Well, why don't you tell me what you *can* remember?" Terra offered. "Maybe saying it out loud will help." It would also give her a better idea of who he was.

After a moment of silence, her dragon man let out another long breath and nodded again. "All right."

He tilted his head back to the headrest. After a few more moments, he started rambling. The words came out slowly. Only fragments of stories at first, but the longer he went on, the longer his stories got.

His life sounds interesting. Most of it was either him in dragon form or centered around training of some type. "Were you in the military?" Terra asked.

The dragon man pulled himself from his thoughts and looked at her. "No." He shook his head. "Not the military, and not the police, but something." He raised his hand to his head as if it pained him.

Terra reached her hand over and rested it on the blanket over his leg. "At least you remember something," she tried to comfort him.

He dropped his hand down over hers. "Yes." Leaning his head back, he closed his eyes again. "But it's all pictures and feelings. There is no sound to any of it."

The soft slide of his thumb across Terra's skin sent tingles up her arm. She hadn't meant for him to hold her hand, but now that he had it, she didn't want to pull it away. Giving in to her strange desires, she rolled her hand over and laced her fingers together with his. "I'll help you get through this," she promised. She couldn't very well leave him as he was.

The dragon man drew in a deep breath and let it rush out from him, then squeezed her hand. "Thank you." Rolling his head over, he stared at her. "For everything."

There it was again. That odd wash of desire passed through her again.

Terra stole a quick glance at him. His eyes were just as beautiful now as they had been as a dragon. She would have loved to look at them longer, but she had to pay attention to the road. *Later.* She would find a time later to really study them. Then maybe she could figure out what to call that amazing mix of colors. Hazel just didn't cut it.

Unsure of how to respond to him or to the feelings swirling through her, she simply drove on as he held and caressed her hand. When the silence got too intimate for her, she gave him another quick glance. The look in his eyes heated her insides more than anything her last three boyfriends had done. *And that was just a look.*

Clearing her throat, she broke into the silence with the first thing that popped into her head. "So… What type of clothing do you want?" *Stupid. Stupid. Stupid.* Of all the dumb things she could have picked to break the silence with, she had to pick the one thing that reminded them both that he was naked. She glanced back over at him. A grin had slid across his face.

"At this moment, anything would be better than what I'm wearing," he teased.

With a quick turn of the head, she shot him a dirty look. "Are you dissing my handmade quilt?" she sassed back.

"I would never dream of it."

The fake innocent tone he took made Terra laugh.

"But seriously, jeans and a T-shirt will be fine. And I promise, as soon as I find out who I am, I *will* pay you back."

Another laugh bubbled out of her. "I'm not worried about it." She gave him another glance. "So…" She bit her lip and jumped into the question now pulling at her mind. *To hell with caution and propriety.* "Boxers or briefs?"

He chuckled. "I don't remember," he said and gave her an amused smile. "Why don't you pick, and we'll see how it goes." His smile took on a naughty edge. "Of course, if I don't like them, I could always go without."

The blush that had been hinting at Terra's cheeks flamed into life. *Oh good Lord!* Even if the man couldn't remember anything else, he certainly remembered how to flirt.

Luckily, they didn't have much farther to go until they reached the store. She hated to do it, but she pulled her hand from his so she could turn into the parking lot. Picking a spot away from the building, she pulled in and killed the engine. At least he would have a little bit of privacy while she went inside. Biting her lip, she turned to look at her dragon man. There were so many ways she could respond to his suggestion, but all of them were inappropriate and would likely get her into more trouble than she was already in. And she was already in trouble. Deep. But then again, an inappropriate response could make for a very entertaining evening. It was, after all, starting to get late. She chewed on the idea for a moment longer before deciding. *No.* She knew nothing of this man. He could have a girlfriend, or worse, a wife. It was best to keep everything on a more professional level.

"Wait here. I'll be right back." With that, Terra slid from the car and escaped to the safety of the store. For all she knew, he could be trouble just looking for a place to happen.

ALEX LET OUT a long sigh as he watched Terra head into the store. Somehow, he knew it wasn't like him to flirt, but she made it so easy. Leaning his head back against the seat, he closed his eyes and thought about her. The softness of her skin against his. The flash of those blue eyes as she stole glances at him. And how could he forget the soft pink that colored her cheeks and stole his breath away. He could have easily spent hours just staring at her.

She wasn't a beauty by any sense of the traditional views, but she was easy on his eyes. Her soft, brown hair looked as if it had been styled short and left to grow out. Too short to pull back, and too long for the cut. Physically, she was built as he would expect a farm girl to be. Long and lean. She was probably much stronger than she appeared. He couldn't remember if he had a favorite type of girl, but she just became it. The dragon bit of him curled around in contentment at the idea of keeping her.

He slammed that thought down before the roots could grow any more than they already had. There were more important things to worry about right now. Like finding out who he was. For all he knew, he had a girlfriend somewhere. That thought made him pause. No, he didn't have a girlfriend, but that didn't mean he had time to get one now. No, he needed to concentrate on finding out who he was and remembering that important thing he was sure he'd forgotten. Later, there would be time to pursue other interests. And, oh boy, would he enjoy that pursuit.

Chapter 5

Opening the door, Terra slid into the car with her bags. She glanced over at her dragon man resting in the seat. He had tilted his head back against the headrest and closed his eyes. Sound asleep. Terra smiled at him. *Damn, he was good looking. And that little bit of stubble on his cheek made him that much hotter.* Balling her fingers in the bags, she resisted the urge to reach out and feel the coarse hair.

She shook her head, trying to clear it. What in the hell had come over her? Sure he was hot, but she'd met a lot of good-looking guys. That didn't mean she wanted to crawl into their laps and lick their faces. It had to be all the excitement and mystery that went with him. *Yes. That was it.* She was just turned on by the whole idea of what was going on. A strange man without a memory. And naked to boot! She just needed to get her hormones under control so they could solve his problem.

Reaching out, she patted his leg. "Hey."

He drew in a deep breath as he woke up from his nap.

"Here." She held out the bags for him to take.

It took a second for his brain to kick into gear and take the shopping bags from her.

An amused smile slid across Terra's face as she let out a soft laugh. "Listen. I know this trip to the bar is important to finding out who you are, but it's starting to get late and we've both had a really long day." She didn't know how it showed on her, but she could see how the day had worn on him. "What do you say we grab a pizza and find someplace to hole up for the night?" Her stomach rumbled just thinking about food.

A smile spread across his face. "Sure," he answered. "I think food and some rest would be a great idea." Taking the bags, he pushed one of them to the floor.

Terra nodded and started the car up as her dragon man rummaged through a bag. "So, what do you like on your pizza?"

The man looked up from his search and considered Terra's question. "I don't know." Concern crossed his face as he tried to remember. "I guess just get whatever you like, and we'll go from there."

Whatever I like? Terra's grin widened. "All right. One anchovy and jalapeno pizza coming up."

A look of disgust crossed the dragon man's face. "Fish? On pizza? Please, no."

Terra laughed. "All right. How about a large deluxe with everything?"

"Now that sounds reasonable." He nodded. "But you had better make it two."

She glanced at her passenger curiously. "Two larges?" She could feel his eyes run over her as he evaluated her.

"Better make that two larges and a medium."

This drew Terra's full attention. She turned and stared at him openmouthed. "Are you planning on putting away two full pizzas by yourself?" There was no way the two of them could go through that much pizza.

He just shrugged. "What can I say? I'm a dragon." With that, he went back to rummaging in the bag.

Okay… Terra turned her attention back to the road to hunt down a pizza joint. If he could put away two full pizzas in one sitting, she would hate to see what his food bill for a month would be.

"What's this?"

Terra glanced over to see what her dragon man had pulled from the bag.

He held up a pack of low-rise, cotton panties.

Reaching out, Terra shoved the pack back in the bag. "That's my bag!" She yanked the plastic from his hands and shoved it into the back seat.

He snickered. "I was wondering why you had gotten me pink underwear."

Terra shot him a dirty look. Only one pair of the panties was pink. The other two were flowered. "Well excuse me for wanting clean underwear," she huffed. "It's not like I could go home and get any."

The dragon man let out a long sigh. "I'm sorry." Regret was heavy in his voice. "I didn't mean for you to get caught up in my problems." He pulled the blanket back around him tightly.

Nice going, numbskull. "Hey." Terra reached over and dropped her hand on his leg. "I didn't mean to snap at you. I know you didn't mean for any of this to happen." She patted his leg in a comforting way. "We'll figure it out."

A weak, ironic laugh slipped out of him. "At least you can walk away from this any time you want." There was a depressed note in his voice that made Terra's heart clench.

"No." She patted his leg again. "I won't leave you like this." She glanced over to see him staring at her with those beautiful eyes. "I'll help you find the answers you need."

A spark of hope lit his face.

"But first," she said as she pulled her hand from his leg. "Let's see about some food." She turned the car into the parking lot of a pizza place. "I'll be right back." She paused before jumping out of the car and considered him. "Will you be okay here by yourself?" There was something in his posture that made her want to hold him close and tell him everything would be fine.

A slight smile curved up the corner of his mouth. "I'll be fine. Go."

Terra considered him for a moment longer before getting out. It was amazing how fast he had gone from joking to depressed. If he were going to take her teasing so seriously, she would have to watch what she said around him. She was, after all, just getting to know him.

ALEX WATCHED Terra as she disappeared into the building. What the hell was wrong with him? He had just gone from laughing and joking to dark and depressed in a matter of seconds. The mood swing had hit him so fast it left his head spinning. If he didn't know any better, he would have said he was pregnant, or brooding.

That thought made him stop. *Brooding.* He knew that word but couldn't remember what it meant. A flash of scales provided him with the answer his human mind couldn't come up with. It was a time in a male dragon's life where his hormones got out of whack, usually caused by a growth spurt, a female dragon during her fertile period, or when faced with a potential mate.

Alex was sure he was finished growing, so a growth spurt was out of the question. He would've had to have spent a fair amount of time in the presence of a fertile female for that to bring on a brooding, and he didn't think that was the case. So, that left a potential mate. The ads in the window of the shop hid most of the lobby, but Alex could just see Terra waiting in the short line. A feeling of contentment rolled through him.

He closed his eyes and focused on his dragon bit. "She's human," he protested.

His dragon laughed at him. That was a weak argument, and both of his halves knew it.

Taking a human as a mate could be problematic, but there were lots of dragons who did. Dragons tended to live much longer than the average human, but there was something in the magic of bonding and the sharing of a scale that would extend a human mate's life. They would live as long as their dragon did. Why Alex knew this piece of trivia and not his own name irked him. He kept remembering little things, but none of the information he needed.

Turning his eyes away from the woman helping him, he pulled the bag of clothing up from the floor and opened it. While the other bag had female clothing and essentials, this one held male. He ripped open the pack of underwear and pulled out a pair. At least she had gone for the dark-colored briefs and not the plain white ones. It took him a moment, but he shimmied into them. Next came the long-sleeved T-shirt. It was amazingly soft and the same shade of blue as his dragon. Just the fact that she had chosen something in his color made his dragon happy. The pants she had gotten him were a little large in the waist. They would hang low on his hips, but he could make them work.

Now that he was mostly dressed, Alex slipped from the car to go in and help with the food. He also wanted to make sure there weren't any weird misunderstandings between them. His random mood swing had thrown them both.

Pausing in the doorway to the shop, his eyes landed on Terra, and he sighed contently. She stood back from the counter, waiting. Something in her posture told him she was annoyed with the older woman at the counter.

"So, I can't use this coupon?" The woman held out a crumpled piece of paper to the cashier.

He took it and looked at it. "No. This was last month's special." He pointed to the bottom of the ticket where the date was clearly printed on the paper.

"But that was only three days ago," the woman complained. "You can still give it to me for that price."

Alex smiled as he saw Terra's back stiffen with aggravation as the woman argued on. Stepping up behind her, Alex wrapped his arms around her and pulled her back into him. *God, she felt good.* Not quite as good as when he hadn't been wearing clothing, but good nonetheless.

Terra let out a squeak of surprise and turned her head so she could see who'd caught her. "You scared the daylights out of me!" she complained as he hunched over and rested his chin on her shoulder.

"Sorry," he apologized. "I just wanted to come make sure you were okay. Things are a little weird for me at the moment, and, well—"

"I understand." She wrapped her arms up over his and relaxed a little. "You've had a really hard day." She patted his arm reassuringly. "We'll get you through this."

Alex let out a sigh and resisted the urge to kiss her. Even if it was just a thank you kiss on the shoulder. Standing up to his full height, he looked around the shop. Other than a picture of the large head of the shop's mascot, there wasn't anything that could hold his attention away from the woman in his arms. He turned back to her and drew in a deep breath. The smell of cooking pizza masked her scent, but he could just pick up a floral hint from her shampoo. Even that made his toes curl in delight.

Finally, the old woman at the counter had placed her order and stepped away, grumbling about the young clerk cheating her out of her coupons.

Alex let Terra go as she stepped forwards, pulling free of his arms.

She turned to look at him with a question in her eyes.

"I'll be right back." He winked at her and turned towards the bathroom. Now that he was up and moving, he had this undeniable pressure reminding him that he'd slept most of the day.

SHAKING HER HEAD, Terra turned back to the poor, abused clerk and gave him her order. Three large pizzas. One deluxe, one meat lover's, and one cheese. If nothing else, they could have pizza for breakfast in the morning. After tucking her wallet back into her purse, she turned away from the counter and looked around the small shop. The old woman had settled herself on one of the benches, so Terra took a seat on the other.

"Your boyfriend really should be wearing shoes," the woman called to Terra.

Terra turned to look at the complaining woman. "What?" she asked, shocked.

"Your boyfriend." The woman nodded to the bathroom. "He really should be wearing shoes. There's no telling what's on the floor in there."

Terra gaped at the woman. Yes. The woman had just called the dragon man her boyfriend. "He's not my boyfriend." The protest slipped out before Terra thought about it.

The woman huffed. "Well then, he shouldn't be

hanging all over you like that." She pulled her large bag into her lap more and grumbled on. "Back in my day, men respected women in public. And only a child would run around without shoes on."

Terra bit her lip before something scathing came out of her mouth. *How dare this woman complain about my dragon's bare feet? She doesn't know what we've been through today.*

"You will have to pardon my lack of proper attire," the dragon man answered as he came out of the bathroom, wiping his hands on the back of his pants. "As it is, I don't currently own a pair of shoes." He dropped himself onto the bench next to Terra.

The old woman glared at him. "You mean to tell me that you don't have any shoes at all?"

Lacing his fingers across his stomach, the man leaned back in the chair. He stuck his bare feet out in front of him and crossed his ankles. "Nope," he said as if he was proud of that fact. "In fact, if it wasn't for the insistence of this kind lady, I'd be running around naked, too." To emphasize his point, he reached out and pulled the size sticker off the leg of his jeans.

Terra bit the inside of her cheek to keep from laughing out loud.

The old woman looked scandalized at them. "Well, I never!" She got up and stormed out of the shop.

A loud laugh slipped out of Terra as the door swung shut. It had been a real pleasure to see him put the woman in her place. "I can't believe you just did that!" she said as soon as she could get her breath back.

"I'm sure I missed something, but I didn't like how

she was talking to you." The dragon man toyed with the sticker from his pants as he spoke.

Terra smiled at him. He was defending her honor. *How sweet!* She slipped over on the bench until her shoulder bumped into his. "It's okay. She's old and grumpy."

He chuckled and leaned against her. "True, but just because someone's lived a long life doesn't mean they should be telling others how to live."

Curiosity burned at Terra's mind. So many of the dragons that had gone missing were ancient; could her dragon man be just as old as they were?

"How old are you?" The question came out before she could stop it.

The movement of the sticker stopped as he thought about the question. Slowly, he crumpled the plastic up before turning to look at her. "I don't remember." He let out a soft sigh as his eyes drifted back to his curled fingers. Closing his eyes, he drew in several even breaths as he thought. "I have to be as old as she is," he finally said as he looked up at Terra, "if not older."

Sitting up away from him, Terra considered him for a moment. The woman had to have been sixty or seventy years old, but her dragon man didn't look a day over thirty. His eyes held a hint of fear as if he expected her to be appalled by his answer. She shifted back to lean against him again. "As long as you don't get grouchy." *It really doesn't matter how old he is.*

The man chuckled as he slipped his arm around her shoulder and held her closer to him. "I'll try, but I can't promise anything. It may go against my character."

That gave Terra a moment's pause. *They still had to find out who he was.* There was no telling what would happen when they had that information. He would probably go back to his old life and forget about her. That struck a sad note in Terra's heart, but she pushed it away. She would worry about that later. For now, they just had to get their pizza and find a place to rest. Tomorrow, they would worry about finding the past and what that meant for the future.

Chapter 6

"What do you mean, you're out of rooms?" Terra asked again. This was the fourth hotel they'd tried, and no one had anything available.

The look the clerk gave her was apologetic. "There's a comic book convention in town, and everything is booked solid through Monday."

The dragon man placed his hand in the small of Terra's back, calming her down. "Could you check one more time, please?"

The clerk let out an audible sigh and turned his attention to the computer.

Terra glanced up at her dragon man. *Why did his touch have such a soothing effect?* She pondered this as he waited patiently for the clerk to check his records.

A curious noise came out of the clerk as he tapped away on his console. "Well," he said, "it looks like you're in luck. Someone just canceled an online reservation. It looks like we do have one opening."

"Fantastic!" The dragon man smiled at the clerk. "We'll take it."

Terra laughed softly to herself. Her dragon hadn't even bothered to get any of the important information about where they would stay. Pulling out her wallet, she handed her driver's license to the clerk so he could get them registered. Hopefully it wouldn't be too much. She had a decent amount put back, but her mystery man was really hitting her pocketbook hard today.

As if he could sense her reluctance to part with her hard-earned money, the dragon man ran his hand down her back again. He leaned in and whispered softly in her ear. "I'll make sure you get it back."

Terra just snorted out a soft laugh and shook her head, amused. Somehow, she knew that once they had answers, he would do his best to keep his word. She leaned into his side, a silent show of gratitude.

After a few minutes and some paperwork, the clerk handed her a key card. "You're on the fourth floor." He pointed to the elevators at the other end of the lobby.

Thanking him, Terra led the way back to the car to park it and get their things. She was so ready to curl up in a nice, warm bed and crash for the night.

"YOU HAVE GOT to be kidding me," Terra growled as she stood in the entryway and stared into the room.

It was a nice room. There was even a small fridge where they could stow the few slices of pizza they hadn't eaten. But it was the single, small bed that had Terra stopping in her tracks. One bed? *One! And a full-sized bed at the most!* There was no way they could both sleep in that bed together. Okay, so she had seen her dragon man naked on more than one occasion, but that was a long shot from curling up next to him in the same bed. Especially a *small* bed!

A chuckle sounded from behind her as the dragon man looked over her shoulder to see what had made her stop. "Don't worry about it." He leaned in and kissed the top of her head before moving around her and into the room. "You take the bed. I'll sleep on the floor."

Terra stood rooted to the floor. *What! Did he just kiss me?* The thought ran around her brain, shorting it out. Finally, the rest of what he'd said filtered in. That moved her feet.

"You can't sleep on the floor!" She went over and dumped her shopping bags on the bed next to where he was rummaging through his stuff.

"It's not a big deal." The man shrugged. "It's not the first time I've ever slept on the floor. Probably won't be the last."

Pulling the leather bag off her shoulder, she dropped it on the bed and turned towards him. "No." She pushed on his side so he would turn and look at her. "You've had a hard day and need a good night's sleep. Besides, this floor is probably disgusting. You take the bed. I'll sleep in the chair."

The dragon man stared at her for a long moment. His gorgeous eyes locked with hers. "I can't let you sleep in the chair. You've had a hard day, too. You take the bed." His hand came up to her hip as he spoke. The movement drew them closer together.

"I won't sleep, knowing you're on the floor," Terra said, staring up into his face. Desire pulled at her body as the tip of his tongue slipped across his lower lip, dampening it.

"Fine," he breathed the word softly.

Terra's pulse skipped as he raised his hand to the side of her face, drawing her closer to him. Her eyes dropped to his mouth—so close, so kissable. *God, he would be wonderful to kiss.* She nearly leaned in to taste him, when he spoke again.

"We'll share the bed."

A zing of excitement raced through Terra's insides, making her gasp. It might be dangerous to her sanity, but yes, she would share the bed with this man.

"Yes." The agreement slipped from her lips in a breathy whisper.

Her hands settled on his hips, pulling him even closer. Terra wasn't a loose girl by any meaning of the word, but there was just something about this man that made her want to give in without a fight. Even if it was only for one night. She had a feeling this would be the best night of her life. Pressing into his front, she tilted her head back, clearly offering herself up for his kiss.

A shiver raced through him as he pulled her harder against him. The evidence of his arousal was pressed between them, and she could feel his desire racing through him like electricity tingling across his skin. He paused just millimeters away from her lips. His body temperature shot up as he held her, almost panting. Warm puffs of air caressed her face as he breathed.

Closing her eyes, Terra tilted her head and moved to take his mouth. She met with... nothing. Opening her eyes, she found that he was gone. She could still feel the heat from his body, but he wasn't there anymore.

The soft click of the bathroom door drew her attention. She stood there, staring at the closed door. Had he really just escaped to the bathroom? After she had left herself so open for him? Embarrassment raced across her skin. How could she be so stupid? How could she have read the signs so wrong! Of course he'd run. He was way out of her league.

ALEX LEANED against the bathroom door, trying to catch his breath. *Shit!* He'd almost kissed her. And he wouldn't have stopped at just a kiss. He would have had her, in every way he could. And she would have let him. Then, his goose would really have been cooked. His dragon was already on the verge of claiming her. Had he given in to both of their desires, it would have been impossible to stop a bond from forming. He could feel scales rubbing against the inside of his skin, driving him to go out and claim what was his. *No!* He couldn't... *wouldn't* do that to her.

Had he known who he was, his situation in life, he could have let things go on. But, as it was, he couldn't drag her into his life not knowing what he had to offer her. They were already on the run from some strange men that had broken into her house and shot at her. And they were most definitely after *him*, not her.

No. The best thing for him to do at this moment was to beat down that instinct driving him to claim her. Just the fact that he had left her hanging, so obviously ready to take that next step, would drive some bit of a wedge between them. But that was okay. Tomorrow, after they had both calmed down, he would explain the situation to her. Even if that meant he had to admit that he liked her.

Drawing in a deep breath, he closed his eyes and listened to the sounds from the other room. The rustling of plastic and banging of the fridge led him to believe she was well and truly pissed at him. Even the water rushing in the sink as she brushed her teeth sounded bitter. It was her right to be angry at him. He was kind of angry at himself for leaving her like that.

Pulling off his clothes, Alex folded them neatly on the back of the toilet and twisted on the water in the shower as cold as he could stand. Right now, he just needed to get a grip on his hormones, and a cold shower would go a long way to chilling him out. He nearly squeaked when he climbed into the frigid spray.

Grabbing up the hotel soap, he lathered up a washcloth. *Maybe a little pain added in would help.* He scrubbed himself as hard as he could, but it didn't really do much for his mental state. Well, at least he was clean again. Cutting off the water, he climbed out and dried himself off.

What the hell am I going to do now? The cold shower hadn't done much to relieve his arousal. And now he was supposed to go out and face Terra. He thought about her out there in that bed—soft and warm, just waiting for him to come out. Heat raced through his body, making him need another cold shower. Yeah, there was no way he was going to make it through this night.

Alex glanced at his clothing. He could put it back on, but that wasn't much of a barrier. And if his dragon had anything to say about it, the clothes wouldn't stay on very long. A smile slipped across his face as an answer came to him. He would let his dragon win this one.

Hanging the towel up, Alex cracked the door open and let go of his control. Scales rushed over his skin as he shifted into his lesser form. Yes, his dragon would push him to get closer to Terra, but in this form, there was no way they would be tempted to finish what they had started.

Rearing up, he caught the switch with his claw and clicked off the light before nosing out of the bathroom. The room beyond was dark. He hadn't really thought about how long he had been in the bathroom, but obviously, Terra had already gone to bed. Alex slipped out and looked over the room. Sure enough, he could see her all tucked in on the far side of the mattress. Carefully, he slipped past the end of the bed and headed for the armchair. Surely, Terra wouldn't want him in the bed after he had abandoned her like that. It would be tight, but he could curl up on the chair for the night.

"Don't you even dare."

The growled words stopped him from climbing into the seat. Alex turned to look at the form in the bed. He could feel the waves of anger coming off her. He swallowed hard. Maybe he should have just given in to their desires earlier.

"Unless you want me to kick it, get your ass up here. Now."

Lowering his head, he slinked back across the room and around to the open side of the bed.

Terra sat up and flipped the covers back for him.

Feeling guilty, he climbed up and lay down. "I'm sorry," he gurgled.

Terra flipped the covers back over him.

He turned his head so he could watch her out of one eye. "Please don't be mad at me."

She let out a loud sigh and lay back down, facing away from him. "Just go to sleep." Her voice held a sharp note of hurt in it.

Alex swallowed hard and closed his eyes. It took several minutes of arguing with himself to come to the decision to stay in this form for the night. Tomorrow, he would shift back and apologize to her. Somehow, he would find a way to make this up to her.

Chapter 7

Consciousness pulled at Terra's mind as she floated on the edge of an uncomfortable sleep. It was much too hot under the covers. She tried to flip the material back but found she couldn't move. There was something heavy on her. Awareness slammed into her as her brain snapped awake. It wasn't just something heavy *on* her; something very warm was tangled *around* her. There was only one thing it could possibly be. Her fingers shifted under the covers to touch the hot object behind her. She hoped to meet with hard scales, but what she felt was a lot softer.

At some time during the night, her dragon had shifted back into a man and wrapped himself around her. And it wasn't just an arm draped over her. Oh no. He had both his arms wrapped around her middle, and his leg was slipped between hers. Now that she was awake, she could feel his breath tickle across her skin from where he had buried his face in her hair at the back of her neck. And somehow, he had managed to work her shirt up to an almost indecent level. His fingers lay splayed across the bare skin over her ribs. Just a slight shift upwards would have him palming her breast. The thought of his fingers on her brought those rosy tips to hard points, and she shut that thought down as fast as she could.

Terra drew in a deep breath, trying to calm the fluttering of her heart. *Talk about mixed signals.* Last night, he had made it very clear he wasn't interested in her. As if leaving her hanging weren't enough, he had shifted in the bathroom so he wouldn't have to explain himself. Then, he had even tried to sneak off to the chair instead of taking his side of the bed. Now what was she supposed to do?

Turning her head, she tried to peek over her shoulder at the sleeping man, but he was pressed into her so hard that she couldn't turn far enough. And speaking of hard, there was definitely something solid pressing into her back. She should have just let him sleep in the chair. Closing her eyes, she relaxed back into his grip. It really wasn't that bad being caught by him. Honestly, it was quite nice waking up being held. She wiggled a little, trying to get more comfortable.

A growl sounded from behind her, and her dragon man buried his face deeper into her hair, if that were even possible. He also tightened his grip around her as he took a deep breath.

Terra froze, waiting to see what he would do.

He let the air out in a long sigh and went back to the deep, even breaths of sleep.

Letting out the air caught in her own lungs, Terra

decided it was time to get up. After what had happened last night, it was probably best for both of them if she wasn't in his arms when he woke up. Especially with the evidence of his arousal pressed so firmly into her back. He was probably dreaming of some leggy blonde with big boobs. Having him wake up to find it was just her would be rather disappointing, and she didn't know if she could handle that type of rejection again.

She pushed against his arms, hoping to move them, but they held her fast. Like solid steel bands.

He let out another growl that froze her.

Geez, it was like someone was taking away his favorite toy. Sighing, Terra glanced over her shoulder again. It looked like she wasn't going to be able to get free without waking him up.

"Hey, Cookie," she whispered, using the nickname she had given his dragon when they'd fled her home.

He growled again.

She patted his arm, trying to wake him up. "Wake up, Cookie."

"I'm not Cookie," he growled, but his hold never loosened.

Irked, Terra tried to shoot him a glare, but she still couldn't turn far enough. "Then what the hell am I supposed to call you? I can't go around calling you 'hey you' all the time." She squirmed in his hold, to no avail.

"Anything but Cookie," he grumbled. Letting out a long sigh, he relinquished his grip.

Terra took the opportunity and climbed out of bed and away from him before he could clamp back down on her. She yanked her shirt back down into place before turning to face him. "You have issues, buddy," she growled as she stormed over and grabbed up her bag of clothing. Right now, she wanted to put as much distance between them as possible. A nice shower should help clean him from her mind. As if she could forget the exquisite feel of him against her skin. Damn it, if he hadn't made his position clear last night, she would have spent the morning rocking his world.

THE SOUND of the bathroom door closing between them broke Alex's heart. Yes, he did have issues, and she didn't know the half of it. He should have just come to bed as a human last night. At least then he could have kept on his clothing... or at least part of them. But no, he had come to bed in his lesser form, thinking that would save them from more awkwardness. How stupid could he be! Of course, his instincts would have shifted him into the form that was best for the situation, and his instincts were pushing him to claim Terra. Therefore, human was the form he had taken while asleep. There had to be a special level of hell where people liked to torture themselves with denied pleasures, because that's where he found himself this morning. God, she had felt good in his arms.

A shiver ran through his body at the sound of the shower turning on. She was there, just feet away from him, getting naked. It was all he could do not to get up and follow her. He rolled onto his back and stared at the ceiling, trying not to envision her soft skin glistening with water. Maybe if he went in and begged, she would forgive him for his stupidity. But, then again, doing that would put him right back at the point where he had been last night. If he let his desires control his actions, he could easily do something that they might both regret later. When dragons chose a mate, it was for life. Alex let out a long sigh as he thought about that. Sex didn't automatically mean a mating bond was formed, but he just knew if he gave in, there would be lasting consequences to the choice.

The door to the bathroom creaked open.

Alex froze as Terra stepped out and laid his pile of clothing on the corner of the bed. Now was his chance to apologize and explain himself. He opened his mouth to speak, but nothing came out. He hadn't looked at her when she had extracted herself from his arms this morning. *Wow!* What a sight he had missed. He must have made some kind of sound because she stood there staring at him like she was expecting him to say something, but he couldn't get two brain cells to bump into each other. She was stunning, standing there in that rumpled shirt and mussed-up hair. *Absolutely beautiful!*

Silence filled the room as he just sat there, staring at her.

Finally, she just shook her head and turned back to the shower waiting for her.

Letting out another long sigh, he dropped himself back to the bed. *Blew it again.* Dragging his sorry carcass from the bed, he went to the pile of clothing she had brought out. He was so screwed. There was no way for him to win, and he knew it. Fighting with his desire was making them both miserable, but giving in could also make them both miserable. There was no good choice either way. *Well crap.*

Alex pulled on his clothing and hated the way it felt against his skin. Even though the shirt was soft, it itched beyond belief. A quick flicker from his dragon told him why. He *was* brooding, and things wouldn't get any better for him.

Pissed at himself, he yanked open the small fridge and pulled out what was left of the pizza. Maybe something in his stomach would help settle his mood. He stared at the four slices left and couldn't bring himself to take one. He could have eaten all four and still been hungry, but that would mean Terra wouldn't get any. He warred with himself for a moment before dropping the box on the bed with the food untouched. His dragon side was too strong. The needs of a potential mate came first. In everything.

Irritated, he went over and dropped himself in the chair to wait for her to come out.

THAT WAS *the worst shower ever!* Terra ran the towel over her hair once again before folding it and hanging it over the towel bar. The actual shower hadn't been that bad, but it was the subject matter she couldn't get out of her mind that bothered her. When she had taken the dragon man's clothing out to him, he hadn't even thanked her. Just lay there on the bed, staring at her with those gorgeous eyes—eyes that held a hunger that had melted her to the core. Had he said something, anything, she would have forgiven him for everything and fallen into his arms. But he hadn't said squat.

Jamming her things into her plastic shopping bag, she scooped it up and headed out to face him. It took everything she had to muster up the courage to open the door. Why did he have such a profound effect on her?

The air in the room was still, and for a moment, Terra thought he had left. Her eyes found him lounging in the chair, watching her. Even from there, she could tell his muscles were tense. She paused in the small entryway and stared at him.

After a moment, he nodded towards the bed. "Eat." The word was not a suggestion.

Terra glanced down at the open pizza box. The four slices of pizza from last night were there, waiting for her. She looked back at him. The expectant look in his eyes irritated her.

"I'm not hungry."

She turned her nose up at the open box and moved to put her stuff down on the small desk. Terra watched out of the corner of her eye as the effects of her words hit him. He actually bristled with rage. *What the hell did he have to be angry about?* She listened to him draw in a few deep breaths before standing up. Tension ran through her muscles as she prepared to defend herself. She had learned her lesson once with angry men, and she was not about to let another beat on her without a fight.

"I'm sorry I snapped at you." His words were much more cordial than before, but they were still a bit clipped. "We have a long day ahead of us. Won't you please have something to eat?"

Well, that was somewhat better. Terra considered him and his suggestion as some of the tension eased from her. Cold pizza didn't sound like a very appetizing breakfast. "I'd rather not."

She turned away from him to gather the rest of her things from the sink but kept an ear open, listening for his reaction. She had seen this cycle before. It was when she and Derrick had first gotten together. He would get upset by something she'd done and try to calm down before exploding at her. Terra held her breath, waiting for the rush of anger from the dragon man.

His response surprised her. He laughed. Turning back, she looked at him, confused by his reaction. He stood there smiling like he was the happiest man on earth. Or an idiot.

"Then would you care to go down and see what they're offering as the complementary continental breakfast?"

Who was this man, and what had he done with the angry one she had just turned her back on? *Wow!* He went up and down faster than a high-bounce rubber ball in a steel room. She considered his offer for a moment before answering. A continental breakfast sounded much better than cold pizza. "Yes."

"As my lady wishes."

Terra stared at him, dumbfounded, as he gathered up their things in record time and went to get the door for her. She stood there, shocked by his actions. She hadn't brushed her teeth or her hair. Hell, she didn't even have her shoes on. A quick glance around showed that he had those in his hand, too.

Irked, she went over and took her things from him, then turned back into the room. "Give me a minute." She dropped her bag on the bed and pulled out her brush and socks, glaring at him when he had the audacity to chuckle.

"My apologies," he said as he let the door swing shut, closing off the outside world. "I guess I'm just a little messed up this morning."

Terra glared at him more as she sat on the bed and pulled her socks on. "A little?"

This brought another laugh from him. "Maybe more than a little."

Nodding, she slipped her feet in her shoes and ran the brush through her damp hair as she considered the man patiently waiting for her. In the matter of a few minutes, he had gone through a whole spectrum of emotions. Maybe he had hit his head harder than she'd thought.

Once her hair was straight, she dropped the brush in the bag and picked it up. Turning to him, she considered him again. "How are you today?"

A smile spread across his face. "I'm up and down right now, but I'm all right."

Yeah, up and down like a yo-yo. Terra watched him closely for a moment more before heading over to the door. "Let's go."

He opened the door and let her lead the way into the hall.

There was something strange going on with her

mystery man, and it wasn't just the fact that he had lost his memory. She watched him out of the corner of her eye as he swung his bags merrily. He even hummed a bit off tune. When they got to the elevators, he stepped up and pressed the button before she could reach it. She turned to look at him fully. For some reason, he looked way too happy.

"Where's the pizza?" she asked when she noticed the missing box.

"It didn't please you, so I left it."

"What?" she asked, shocked. *He didn't just say that, did he?*

"I left it," he said again, "but it doesn't matter. We're on our way to get breakfast."

Terra stood with her mouth open. Had he really said that he'd left it because it didn't *please* her? *What the hell?*

When the elevator door opened, the dragon man ushered her inside and hit the button to go down. Terra stared at him as his happy movements stilled.

"Listen." He cocked his head and gave her a side-long look. "About last night…"

This shut Terra's gaping mouth. The pain of his rejection boiled up in her, and she turned her eyes to the door. "You don't need to explain about last night. I understand perfectly. I can take a hint." Her jaw locked up against her anger.

"*No.*" He practically yelled the word as he turned on her.

Before she could respond to his sudden movement, he had her pinned against the wall. There was an over-whelming need in the way his mouth pressed to hers.

She gasped in surprise, and he took advantage of her parted lips to deepen the kiss. Warmth raced through her as desire melted her in his arms.

Rubbing his hands down her sides, he worshiped at her lips. She moaned softly as his tongue sought out hers, rubbing against it in a very carnal dance that left nothing to her imagination.

The plastic bag with her things slipped from her fingers as she raised her hands to hold him to her. Suddenly, the rejection from last night didn't seem so important. She held on as his hands slid farther down her sides to her hips. They paused there for a moment before slipping lower. Grabbing her thighs, he hefted her up so she was pinned between him and the wall of the elevator. The hard length of his arousal pressed into her as he ground his hips against her, fitting them together as much as their clothing would allow. Heat pooled low in her body as she tugged him closer, needing more from him.

The high-pitched ping of the elevator door rang out, and Terra yanked her head back from him, gasping for breath. The door slid open on the ground floor, but he ignored it as he trailed a line of kisses down the side of her neck and onto her collarbone.

Ignoring the heat and need racing through her, Terra pushed against his shoulders. The door of the elevator stood wide open for anyone to step in if they wanted to. They were going to get caught!

Slowly, he pulled back and looked at her. The pupils of his eyes had gone from being round to the almond shape of a cat's. He blinked a few times before closing his eyes and leaning his head forwards to rest against hers.

"I'm sorry," he whispered as he tried to get his breathing back under control. "I should not have done that." Carefully, he released his grip on Terra's thighs and let her slide down until her feet rested on the floor.

She held on to him, unsure if her legs would support her. *Wow!* There wasn't just desire in that kiss. There was passion and a need that Terra didn't understand. It pulled at her, wanted her. It terrified her.

Slowly, her dragon man's hands came up to her shoulders, and he pushed himself back from her. "Without knowing who I am, I don't have anything to offer you." He opened his eyes and stared at her. His pupils were still slitted like a cat's.

Terra stared at them. *No. Not cats' eyes. Dragons' eyes.* His dragon was staring out of his eyes at her.

Reluctantly, he released her and turned to pick up the things they had dropped. "Forgive me my error," he said softly. "Relationships with dragons are more complicated than with others." He tucked both of their bags into one hand and turned towards her. "We have to be more careful when choosing partners. Dragons mate for life." He held out his free hand to her.

This bit of news shocked her. No wonder he had rejected her last night. How could she blame him for it? If one bout of sex could tie you to someone for life, she sure as hell would want to know who her partner was before banging him. But, then again, there were celebrity dragons that had partner after partner.

"From sex?" she asked as she took his hand.

He chuckled and pressed the button for the lobby again. "No. But sex can have a lot to do with it." When the door opened back up, he pulled her into the lobby. "Securing a mating bond is a complicated process, but it starts with an act of emotional intimacy. And there aren't many things as intimate as a really good orgasm."

Terra had to hand it to him there. If done properly, a good bout of sex would bring people closer together. She had never really stopped to think about how bonding the experience could be.

"So you can't have sex?" With the way he responded to her in the elevator, she was sure he was far from virginal, but one could never make assumptions on those things.

The noise he made in his chest confirmed her thought. *Oh, he had been there many times!*

"I enjoy sex as much as the next man." He found a table in the small breakfast area and placed her in a chair as he talked. "But casual sex with a potential mate can lead to... lasting issues." Dropping their things on the chair next to her, he released her hand, then pulled off the leather bag and placed it on the floor next to the chair. "Wait here, and I'll bring you breakfast." With that, he turned and left her at the table with their things.

Wait, what? Terra stared at the dragon man's back as he went over to the bar and pulled out two plates. *What the hell was going on?*

Her mind ran over the conversation again and again. Okay, so she understood that casual sex was out, but what was this whole deal about a mate? She considered him and his calm façade as he filled the plates with choice bits from the bar. *What was wrong with him?* They had just had one of the most passionate moments in her life… in an elevator. She was still all messed up inside, but he was amazingly serene. *And what was the deal with his eyes?*

He came back over with two heaping plates of food.

Terra's eyes widened as he set one down in front of her. There was no way she was going to make it through all of that.

"Juice or coffee?" he asked.

Looking up, Terra met his gaze. "Both." His eyes were still weird.

He nodded and went to get their drinks.

Still confused, Terra watched him until he returned. "What's going on?" she asked.

Sitting down, her dragon man raised a questioning eyebrow at her.

Terra raised her hand in the air and waved it around. She wanted an explanation for everything, but she didn't know how to voice the question. Apparently, her movement was enough for her dragon man to get the idea.

He smiled and nodded to her plate. "Why don't you eat, and I'll try to explain."

Agreeing, Terra picked up her fork and started into her food.

Chapter 8

A wave of pleasure rippled through Alex as he watched Terra take that first bite of food. He closed his eyes, trying to contain the feelings washing through him. It wasn't the fact that he found enjoyment in watching her eat; it was the fact that he had just fulfilled one of the basic needs of his instincts—providing for his mate. And right now, his instincts were riding him hard.

Drawing in a deep breath, Alex opened his eyes back up and looked around. He always loved the way the world looked when he was in dragon form, but this was the first time he had seen it that way in human form. His dragon was so close to the surface that it would take nothing to pop out scales. Just that passing thought sent a ripple along his shoulders and down his arms. It was probably a good thing that Terra had gotten him a long-sleeved shirt. A half transformation like he was experiencing usually signaled some form of mental break. Had anyone seen the blue tint to his skin, they would have been on the phone to the authorities, and he didn't have time for that now. There were more important things to do, like telling Terra what she needed to know. Only then would his dragon back down again.

"How familiar are you with dragons?" Alex asked. He could almost see her thoughts swirling as she considered how to answer him.

"Not very." She set her fork on the table, waiting for him to continue.

Two long sections on his back itched as his dragon pushed against his skin. "Please eat, and I'll explain."

Terra gave him a pointed look but picked up her fork again.

The itching along his back subsided. He needed to get himself back under control before things got really bad. And it started with telling her everything.

"Dragons are complicated creatures. We are blessed with rational minds, but we are also driven by instincts. And that can give us issues from time to time." He pulled his glass of juice over and rolled it between his hands so his fingers would have something to do while he talked. "Every dragon has three forms; a grand form, a lesser form, and a human form. While we can switch between them at will, it's very rare for the forms to overlap."

"But, your eyes?" She pointed towards him with a forkful of eggs.

Alex looked down at his glass and smiled. Of course she would notice his eyes. He was just lucky no one else had.

"Yes." He looked back up at her. "There are times

when the two sides merge. It's called balance, and it's usually a bad thing. It's a sign of mental instability."

Tension ran through Terra, making her sit taller in her chair.

"Relax," he soothed her. "A dragon can also enter into balance when there is a major split between their two halves. Say, if the dragon wants something, but the human half won't give in. If the want or need is strong enough, the dragon aspect will force its way to the surface, creating a balance—a merging of the two forms."

Carefully, Alex pushed his sleeve up. The tips of blue scales had already pushed their way through his skin.

Terra gasped as he slid his sleeve back into place.

"Don't worry," he tried to soothe her again. "I am stable. I'm just at an impasse. My dragon wants something that I can't give it."

"You haven't seemed very stable to me," Terra huffed as she picked up her juice and drained the short glass.

Alex snickered softly and pushed his untouched juice towards her. "No. I haven't been. But that ties into my current troubles. See, a lot of things in a dragon's life are driven by instinct and hormones. As long as we listen to those little cues, we're fine, but there are times when our systems get upset and we lose those pointers. It leads to wild mood swings and brooding."

"Like when you fall from the sky and get bashed in your head?"

This pulled another soft laugh from Alex. "No. A fall

won't mess with a dragon's system. A growth spurt will. And a female dragon at the peak of fertility will." He paused and considered Terra for a moment before going on. This was the main thing his dragon was pushing him to do. "There is one other thing that can push a dragon into a brooding. Being faced with a potential mate."

All color drained from Terra's face. "I take it you aren't having a growth spurt?"

He chuckled and shook his head. "No."

"Wow." She said the word so softly that he almost didn't hear it. Folding her hands into her lap, she stared at her half-finished food for a moment. Lifting her eyes, she met his gaze. "How come you can remember all this, but you don't remember your name?"

Leaning back in his chair, Alex grinned again. "I don't, but my dragon does."

"Can your dragon tell you who you are?" That was a very sensible question from someone that didn't know anything about dragons.

Alex sighed. "It's told me what I am, but not who. I'm an Elite. I know I've earned the right to use that title, but I don't remember what that means." This point frustrated him to no end. If he could just get two brain cells working together, he was sure he could come up with the answers he needed, but they all seemed to be on different vacations at the moment.

"So, what does your dragon want?" Terra asked timidly.

Alex closed his eyes and drew in a steadying breath, trying to center himself as much as he could, given his messed-up state. Opening his eyes, he gave Terra a pointed look. "It's driving me to claim a mate."

"A mate?" There was a touch of alarm in Terra's voice.

"A girl that it's deemed would fit well into my life."

"Someone you've met recently?"

Alex smiled. Now she was just playing with him. "Very recently."

Just a hint of red crawled up Terra's skin as she looked down and toyed with her napkin. "Maybe someone I know?"

"It's most definitely someone you know." He loved the way she looked with that blush on her skin. "But Terra, here's the problem. I can't pursue anyone until I know what kind of life I could offer."

WOW! This was not how Terra had envisioned the day would go. After being thoroughly rejected by her dragon man, she was sure they would have an awkward day running around, trying to find out who he was. But this was just over the top. To be told that you could possibly be someone's mate was a little disturbing. She hadn't even known him for a full day yet, and most of that time, he had been out cold!

Looking up from her napkin, Terra studied the lines of her dragon man's face. His pupils were still oddly shaped, but now that she was used to it, his emotions were easy to read there. He seemed serene on the outside, but she could tell this whole thing had him severely distressed. Her heart thumped in her chest. It actually hurt to see him in such a state. The idea of being tied to someone she barely knew was frightening, but she couldn't stand the idea of leaving him as he was. She slid her hand out across the table for him to take.

He blinked a few times before lowering his hand to hers.

She squeezed his fingers reassuringly. "Tell me what I can do to help." There was just something about him that made her want to do whatever she could to see him right again.

The dragon man let out a depressed laugh. "Shoot me down." Gripping her fingers tightly, he closed his eyes to wait for the blow.

"What?" Terra asked, shocked. Of all the things she thought he would say, that was not one of them.

He opened his eyes and looked at her again. "Tell me there is no way I stand a chance with you. And mean it." He paused for a second before he went on. "That should be enough of a blow to knock me out of balance and back into a brooding state."

Okay... A complete rejection would settle his system back down. But could she really tell him that and mean it? Did she want to? She had to know more before she made any lasting decisions. "And what happens if I refuse?"

The pupils of his eyes dilated as he drew in a sharp breath. He sat rigid in his seat for a moment before letting out the air very slowly as if he were considering how to respond to her. His mouth moved, and he swallowed before answering.

"Well, that would drop me out of balance, too." He paused and swallowed again. "But it wouldn't do anything to settle down my instincts."

Terra rubbed her thumb over his knuckles as she considered his answer. If she shot him down, he would go back to brooding. Brooding didn't sound like a very pleasant state to be in. For either of them. But, if she didn't, would that mean she was encouraging him? And how would that affect the situation they had found themselves in? He needed her to help him find out who he was, and she wasn't going to leave the poor man helpless. She studied him, weighing her options.

He sat tensely in his seat, waiting for her answer. The skin on the side of his neck was taking on a blue tint. She was going to have to give him an answer very soon before someone noticed his plight. Licking her lower lip, she asked the last thing she needed to know before making her choice. "If I refuse, does that make me your mate?"

The dragon man drew in another long breath and let it out slowly. "No," he answered. "It takes more than that to form a mating bond, but it's a step in that direction." The heated look in his eyes made Terra wiggle in her seat.

She drew her hand away from him and folded it into her lap. "Well then, I guess we had better find out who you are, 'cause I don't think I could shoot you down and truly mean it." Pushing back from the table, she stood up.

The dragon man followed her motion and stood up, too.

"Please," she held her hands out, waving him back to his seat. "Sit back down and eat. I'm just going to the bathroom."

He hesitated for a moment. "Will you be okay?"

Terra laughed out loud, breaking the tension hanging between them. "I'll be fine." She smiled. "Eat your breakfast so we can get moving. We have a long day ahead of us." Turning, she left to find the restroom. She wasn't sure if she wanted to be a dragon's mate, but turning the man down before she found out what life with him would be like just didn't seem right. Only time would tell if they could work it out together.

ALEX WATCHED Terra walk away before settling back into his seat. Closing his eyes, he let out a long sigh. His skin itched as his dragon withdrew, contented with the answer she had given him. He stood a chance, and that was all his dragon wanted—a chance. Opening his eyes, he found that his vision had returned to normal.

Looking at his untouched food, he picked up his fork and pulled the plate closer to himself. Now that she had eaten, he was free to consume as much as he liked. Unfortunately, the answer she had given did nothing to clear the main conflict running around in him. He still didn't know who he was, and that did a lot to curb his appetite. Forcing himself to eat, he considered what course to take from here. They still had to go to the pub and find out if anyone knew who he was. But now he also had to deal with his dragon chasing after Terra. That was going to add a whole new layer of interesting to everything else going on.

Alex was nearly finished with his food when a tingle of electricity raced up his spine. He sat up and turned his head just enough to see Terra walking back into the room. *Great...* Since she hadn't rejected him, his dragon had tuned itself into her. He tracked her as she crossed the dining area and settled back into her seat. Warmth radiated through him as his dragon settled down contently, draining the excess tension from him. *Wonderful!* He hadn't even noticed that his dragon had been alert, waiting for her return. He almost wished she had turned him down and left him to brood. It wouldn't have made life much easier, but brooding was something he was used to.

A rumble of anger echoed up from his chest as his dragon disagreed with that thought.

Terra's eyebrows went up in surprise.

The corner of Alex's lip turned up in a wry smile. "Sorry. I'm still having an argument with myself." He dropped his fork to his plate and slid it away from him. He really did need to get himself back under control.

Terra eyed the few bites he hadn't finished before looking up and considering him. "Are you all right?"

"No, but I will be," he reassured her. "I just need some time to work things out." He paused and let out an ironic laugh. "Well, that and my memories."

Oh yes, he needed his memories. Hopefully, most of

his immediate problems would be solved when he redis-covered who he was.

She snickered softly. "Then how about we get started on that right now?" Picking up her purse, Terra fished her phone out. "So, what was the name of that place?" she asked as she slid her thumb across the screen, unlocking it.

Alex smiled at her and started collecting the used dishes. "The Dragon's Wing." The name felt right coming out of his mouth, like he had said it many times but just couldn't remember it.

Terra clicked away at her phone for a moment. "It's on the other side of town, but I think we can find it." She looked up at him. "Are you ready?"

"In just a moment." Standing up, Alex took the dirty dishes over to the plastic tub waiting for them. He turned around just in time to see Terra slip his leather bag over her shoulder and tuck her purse inside. The motion made him smile. He had forgotten all about that satchel.

"I'll take those," Alex said as he reached out and gently took the plastic bags before she could get a proper grip on them.

She gave him a confused look. "Are you sure?"

He chuckled again. "I'm sure." He slid his hand to her lower back and pressed on it, steering her towards the exit. "It wouldn't be right to let my lady carry every-thing." An ironic smirk slipped across his face. "You haven't turned me down yet, so now I'm going to try to convince you that I would be a good mate."

The note of sarcasm in his voice made Terra look up at him, concerned. "But, I thought you said you couldn't do that until you regained your memories?"

Alex chuckled wryly. "Yes. I did." A forlorn sigh slipped out of him as they walked. "But that doesn't mean that my instincts are going to back off and just let things be. My dragon sees you as a potential mate; therefore, it demands that you be treated as such. But don't worry. It isn't as bad as you think."

"Really?" Terra asked as Alex skirted around her and opened the door before she could put her hand on it.

Alex smiled at her as she paused before heading through the door. "Yes," he said, trying to reassure her. He paused to choose his words carefully, not wanting to come straight out and explain all the little things his dragon was pushing him to do. As it was, he was having a hell of a time trying to resist most of his urges. A quick glance at her face told him she had some doubts.

"Let me see if I can explain." He moved back to her side. Placing his hand on her back again, he guided her out into the parking lot. "Male dragons treat their mates with reverence."

Terra shot him another doubtful look. "Reverence? As in worshipped?"

Definitely not the right word to use. It didn't look like Terra liked the idea of being worshipped.

"I wouldn't say that." Alex tried to think of better way to explain it to her. "Females are treated with respect. They're cared for and protected. Newly bonded and courting males tend to pamper their chosen female."

"Pamper?"

The note of intrigue in Terra's voice curled the corner of Alex's mouth. "Yes," he answered, stroking his hand down the small of her back. The feel of her under his hand made him want to draw her closer, but he resisted the urge. This conversation would go a lot smoother if he gave her space to think. He glanced down to watch her worrying her bottom lip with her teeth. Obviously, she was considering his words hard.

"And how long does this usually last—" She glanced up at him as she spoke. "—the pampering?"

Alex smiled again. "For some, their instincts settle down shortly after the mating bonds are made, but I know old dragons that still spoil their mates. I guess it just depends on the dragon."

They walked the rest of the way to the car in silence as Terra thought, and he prayed he hadn't just scared her off.

Once settled into the car, Terra looked over at him, another question floating in her eyes. "Do female dragons go through this?"

Alex cocked his head as he considered his answer. "Female dragons don't go through the same urges that the males do. They don't brood, but they do have moments when their fertility peaks. Thankfully, that only happens a few times in their life. They tend to get a little crazy. Plus, the overproduction of pheromones can send the males around them into a brooding. It's not fun to see."

"Oh."

Alex watched as Terra turned her attention back to the car. The look on her face was thoughtful. Alex relaxed back into the seat to let her think. Hopefully, the truth hadn't scared her off the idea of being his mate. But only time would tell.

Chapter 9

The Dragon's Wing was like no other place Terra had ever been. It was easy to find if you were looking for it, but it was also far enough out of town that people wouldn't just stumble across it while out looking for a good time. A hand-carved sign held a green dragon curled around the name of the pub. If they hadn't been watching for it, they could have easily mistaken the old building for the barn it had once been.

"Do you know this place?" Terra asked as she pulled into the parking lot and killed the engine. The look on her dragon man's face told her he was working through his scrambled memories, but things most definitely clicked into place as he studied the tall building.

He leaned forwards and placed his hand on the dash as he stared out the windshield. "Yes."

He breathed the word so softly Terra almost missed it. *Well, that answer was promising.*

"Then let's go see if they can tell us who you are."

Pulling her keys out of the ignition, Terra got out of the car. She pulled the dragon man's leather bag out and slung it over her shoulder. With the awed look on his face, there was no way her mystery man would remember the thing on his own. Since there was plenty of room in the bag, she dropped her purse back in so she would only have to keep up with one bag.

Climbing from the car, her dragon man met her at the front of the car. His eyes ran over every inch of the rustic building. "I know this place." His words held a note of wonder to them.

Terra looked up at the pub. The foundation and ground floor of the old barn were done up in river rocks. Long, wooden planks ran vertically up the sides, holding up a high, A-frame roof.

"Come on." Reaching out, Terra grabbed the man's hand and pulled him towards the door set in the center of the building.

A soft laugh crept out of him, and he hurried to catch up to her. He slipped his arm around her shoulder, tucking her to his side.

Terra enjoyed the feel of him around her, but the conversation they'd had over breakfast played in the back of her mind. *Males pamper their mates.* Was this a part of that? Should she stop him until they found out who he was? Did she want to? She shook her head and squished that line of thought. There would be time enough to deal with that once they had answers to the mystery of who he was.

Stopping at the heavy wooden door, he pulled it open and let Terra lead the way in.

The door opened into a very small foyer. Three or four people might have been able to fit in the area, but only if they were close friends. Terra looked around at the walls. They were covered in old tin advertisement signs nailed into the wooden walls. *Very rustic.* The dragon man stepped into the area behind her, and a bell chimed as the door clicked closed.

Terra moved forwards to see into the main room. It was cozy. Small oil lamps sat at the center of each table, adding to the natural light that flowed in through the windows. There were a few people scattered around, but overall, it was fairly quiet for a bar.

"Hello," a cheerful voice called from the right.

Terra turned towards the sound.

A young woman with a high ponytail bounced towards them. "Just one?" she asked.

The dragon man stepped up behind Terra so the waitress could see him. "Two," he answered.

"*Lex!*" The young woman bounced harder. "God, we were so worried with the way you took off out of here yesterday. Was everything okay with Melanie?"

The name struck a chord with Terra. It took her a moment to drag up where she had heard that name before. *Melanie. That was the name of the last dragon in the file.* Terra glanced up at her mystery man and watched as confusion and concern raced across his face.

"I don't remember," he said softly and raised his hand up to touch his head as if it hurt. Closing his eyes, he rubbed his temple.

The young woman stopped her excited bounce and cocked her head in concern. "Alex, are you all right?"

She reached her hand out towards him. Just before she touched him, she stopped and curled her fingers up.

"Yes," the man said as he shook his head no.

The waitress pulled her hand back and stared at him in confusion.

"He's had a long day," Terra said, breaking into the building tension.

She looked up at her mystery man. *Alex*. That name fit him well. At the moment, he looked rather pale. Terra turned her attention back to the waitress.

"Could we possibly have someplace to sit down and get some water?"

The question startled the woman back into her job. "Yes. Of course. This way." She turned and led them deeper into the pub.

Reaching out, Terra laid her hand on Alex's arm. "Come on." She drew him into the main room and pushed him after the waitress with a hand on his back.

Alex nodded and went where she directed him.

There weren't very many people in the pub, but every eye was on them as Terra pushed Alex through the tables. She glanced around at the faces. Hadn't they ever seen someone in pain before? Or maybe he wasn't one to accept help. Terra thought back to the way the waitress had stopped before she touched him. Terra rubbed her fingers in the soft material at the small of his back. Could it be the fact that she was touching him? Maybe her dragon man wasn't the touchy-feely type. Terra looked up at him. *That couldn't be.* Her dragon man had never had any qualms about touching her. He seemed to like it. She definitely did.

Seeing where her thoughts were leading, Terra shook her head slightly. There were more important things to think about right now. Like figuring out who her dragon man was. Terra gave her head another soft shake. She had to stop thinking of him as 'her dragon man'. Now that she knew it, she really needed to think of him using his name. *Yes. He's Alex now.*

CLOSING HIS EYES, Alex trusted Terra's soft touch to guide him through the pub. He needed a moment to collect himself after the young woman had stirred his memories. A rush of images had overwhelmed him as a mess of things came back to him at once. They jumbled over one another, all demanding to be seen. A hushed conversation in a secluded corner table. The rush of air over wings. The breaking of glass. A sense of dread. The tingle of electricity over scales. Each more important than the last, and each just a ghost of what the full memory should have been.

"Hey."

Terra's soft voice and the feel of her hand on his back pulled Alex out of his thoughts. He opened his eyes to look at the booth where the waitress had led them. It was familiar. He had been here. Many times. A flash of memory hit, and he reached out and grabbed onto the tabletop. Terra's hand gripped him as he swayed on his feet.

"Let me go get you that water." The young woman

leading them turned to hurry off but stopped and looked back. "Or would you rather have the usual?"

The usual? With random memories churning through his brain, Alex couldn't recall what his usual was. "Please," he answered. Just trying to think of what he usually got made him want the unknown substance.

"Make it two," Terra called to the waitress.

The young woman nodded and left.

"Come on." Terra tried to pull Alex over and put him into one of the bench seats, but he shook his head.

Wrapping his arm around the woman helping him, Alex ushered her into the bench seat ahead of him. "Please sit."

Terra paused for a moment before sliding into the seat. She scooted over against the wall as he slid into the seat next to her.

Dropping his head to the table, Alex cushioned it on his hands to sort through the images flashing through his head. They raced around so fast that he couldn't make heads or tails of them. The only thing he could under-stand was a sense of loss and urgency, but there was no context as to what he had lost or what was so urgent. Alex opened his eyes for a moment as he felt Terra's fingers start to rub the tension from the back of his neck and shoulders. Closing them again, he relaxed as she worked.

"Are you all right?" she asked softly.

Alex drew in a long breath. The feel of her fingers working into his tight muscles calmed the swirling memories, but not enough for him to recognize any of them. He let the air out slowly before opening his eyes and sitting up. "Not really," he answered honesty. "But it's getting better."

Terra slid her arm over and around his back. She leaned into his side, holding him to her. "We'll figure it out."

A soft chuckle slipped out of Alex. Yes, they would figure it out. He finally knew who he was again. *Alex.* That name fit him much better than the 'Lex' the waitress had called him. But even Lex fit him better than Cookie. And if he were lucky, the young woman bringing the drinks would be able to fill in some other missing information.

"Alex!" a deep, male voice called to him.

Alex turned to look at the stout man carrying two mugs in one hand and a leather jacket in the other.

"Michele said you were here." The man set the two mugs on the table and hooked a chair from another table nearby. He swung it around and plopped down into it backwards. The chair creaked under the man's weight.

The smell of dragon musk hit Alex, driving a rumble from his chest. Something about the man was very familiar, but the instinct to protect his mate from the new suitor drove him to lean forwards, blocking the man's view of Terra.

Alex's protective move raised the man's eyebrows in surprise.

Pulling back her arm, Terra smacked Alex in the shoulder, grabbing his attention. "Stop being rude," she scolded him.

Alex twisted to stare at Terra, surprised by her

actions. Didn't she know that he was protecting her? He studied the cross look on her face before closing his eyes to concentrate. No, she didn't realize he was protecting her. All she saw was him hiding her away from someone new. He had to get himself under control. Struggling with his instincts, Alex leaned back in the booth so the new man could see Terra.

"Sorry about that," Terra said. "We've had a long day."

Alex listened closely to the warm note in her voice while trying to hold back his instinct to hide her away from the unknown person.

The man laughed. "Don't worry about it, love. Brooding dragons have a tendency to be a little overprotective. Although, I'm surprised to see this one brooding over anyone."

Alex cracked his eyes and watched as the man held his hand out to Terra.

"I'm Alister Stewert, but the men call me Brigs."

"Terra Watson." Terra reached out and took his hand.

A soft growl rumbled up from Alex's chest.

Pulling her hand back, Terra shot Alex an offended look.

Alex shook his head slightly and forced the sound to stop. Yes, his dragon was trying to claim her, but he needed to get it under control. She still wasn't his mate, and this man, whomever he was, wasn't out to steal her away from him. Humans didn't understand instincts the same way dragons did, and if he didn't cool it, he could easily drive a wedge between them.

To settle the irritation riding him, Alex reached over and pulled one of the cups towards him. It was hot, and the soft aroma of flowers drifted up with the steam. Blowing on the frothy top, he sipped at the pale liquid inside. Sweetened milk flavored with tea rolled across his tongue and soothed his frayed nerves. He remembered this drink. It was relaxing and helped to slow his thoughts so he could process them.

Taking the hot mug with him, he leaned back in the booth and rested the cup against his chest, where he could breathe in the pleasant aroma. Alex listened to Terra and Brigs chat as he let things process through his mind. This had been exactly what he needed to get his memory back. This and a little time.

Chapter 10

Terra stared at Alex for a moment. She vaguely remembered him mentioning that dragons were protective over their mates, but did that mean they were possessive of them, too? She shook the thought away and turned her attention back to the new man. Smiling at Brigs, she ignored Alex as he pulled his cup over to himself. Maybe his drink would chill him out.

"How did you get a name like Brigs from Alister?"

Brigs dropped the leather jacket on the table and folded his arms over the back of the chair. "It comes from the time I spent in the army."

"You were in the army?" Terra glanced over the man. He was a touch on the stout side with neatly trimmed, brown hair and a thin mustache. His voice held a hint of an accent to it, but Terra couldn't place it.

"Aye. But that's a long story." Brigs grinned at her and changed the subject. "So how did you end up with a curmudgeon like Alex here?"

"Curmudgeon?" Terra said as she looked at the man in the booth next to her. He had relaxed back on the bench so he was almost lying down. His cup was cradled on his chest and his eyes were closed. If she didn't know better, she would have sworn he'd fallen asleep. She considered him for a moment. He didn't seem like a surly person.

Brigs shrugged a bit. "Well, maybe not a complete curmudgeon, but he does tend to be a bit antisocial. It's been a while since I've seen him show up anywhere with a lovely lady by his side, let alone brooding. So how'd you manage to catch his attention?"

She glanced between Brigs and Alex, not sure how to take this news. He didn't seem very antisocial to her. In fact, he had been great company. Well, for the hours that he'd been awake, at least. She studied him for a moment, trying to see him as Brigs had suggested, but she couldn't.

"That's also a long story." Terra kept her answer vague, unsure how much information she should give Brigs. They had, after all, been chased out of her home at gunpoint.

"I crashed in her backyard," Alex answered.

Terra stared at him, surprised. "You remember?"

"Bits." Alex sighed and sipped at his drink. "It's coming back."

"Remember?" Brigs asked. His voice held a note of concern.

"He hit his head," Terra said, feeling a little guilty. "He's been having some problems with his memory."

Alex made an irritated noise but didn't say anything else.

"Ah." Brigs shifted in his seat. "And a brooding on top of that certainly wouldn't make things easy."

Alex made another soft noise and sipped at his drink.

"But the tea should help." Brigs chuckled. "It always helps."

"Tea?" Terra asked glancing at the mug Alex clutched to his chest. *What was in his tea?* Reaching out, she pulled her matching cup over and looked into it. White foam covered the top, preventing her from seeing the actual liquid, but there was a thin chain attached to the side of the cup. Picking it up, she sipped at the drink and found it rather pleasant.

"It's a Lo——" Brigs started.

"London Fog," Alex supplied, cutting off Brigs' answer.

Brigs grinned again. "One of the few drinks that will relax an uptight dragon."

"Not uptight," Alex grumbled, but he didn't move.

Brigs laughed again. "Alex, you are one of the most tightly wound dragons I know. But that's what makes you so good at your job."

Another irritated noise came from the man relaxing in the booth, but he didn't move or protest.

Turning his attention back to Terra, Brigs smiled again. "He can get a little caught up in the details, but he's very good at solving problems once you get a cup or two of tea in him."

"Tea?" Terra asked again as she glanced into the

cup. It was definitely some form of milk tea, but it had a floral taste to it that she couldn't place. *Very tasty.*

"Well, not the tea." Brigs shrugged.

"Lavender," Alex supplied the answer.

Terra stared down into her cup. Now that she knew what that floral taste was, she recognized it. "Lavender?" She looked back up to the men.

"Aye. It's one of the few things that will affect a dragon," Brigs explained, nodding towards the relaxed man in the booth. "For Alex, it opens his mind."

"Catnip for dragons," Alex muttered as he took another sip.

Brigs laughed again. "It has been called that." He turned his attention back to Terra. "But you have to be careful with it. A little can help you relax, but a lot can wind you up. And some dragons are more sensitive to it than others."

Alex made a confirming noise in his throat before taking another sip.

"But most know their limits," Brigs added.

Interesting. Terra sipped at the warm tea. "What happens if they get too much?" she asked, glancing over at the way Alex was resting in the booth.

Brigs grinned. "Get three cups in him, and you'll find out." His voice held a hint of mischief to it. "But make sure you don't have anything planned for the rest of the night."

The suggestion in the man's tone surprised Terra. She glanced at Alex again. Did Brigs just imply that lavender would increase a dragon's desires? If that was the case, maybe she should take the cup of tea away from Alex. After that kiss in the elevator and his confession at breakfast, she wasn't sure what would happen if he continued to drink that stuff.

"Alex." The serious tone Brigs took washed all thought out of Terra. "Can you tell me what happened with Melanie yesterday?"

Terra tensed up, waiting to see how Alex answered. Obviously, his crashing in her backyard had something to do with this woman.

Alex sat quietly for a moment before answering. "Not right now."

Brigs shot Terra a glance before nodding. "Do you need me to call Sanders? He's been blowing up everyone's phones looking for you."

An annoyed noise came for Alex. "No. I'll deal with it."

"Well then," Brigs thumped the table gently, "I'll leave you to your tea." He stood up and spun the chair back to the table where it had come from. "Let me know if there is anything I can do."

Alex made another soft noise in agreement, and Brigs turned to leave.

"Oh." The man stopped and turned back. "Since the weather's been bad, we moved your bike to the barn." With that, he turned and left.

Terra watched as Alex raised his hand in acknowledgement. He dropped it back to the seat and sat there, quietly sipping on his tea. She tried not to fidget in her seat as her curiosity grew. It was obvious he remembered something, but she had no idea how much until he decided to say something. And he didn't seem like he was going to say anything at the moment.

"Well?" Terra pushed when she couldn't stand the suspense anymore. "Is it coming back?"

Alex let out a long breath and sat up. "Yes." He set his cup on the table and reached for the leather jacket Brigs had left. "But not fast enough." Digging in the pockets of the coat, he pulled out a phone and a wallet. "Let's see what we can find here." Concern crossed his face when he looked at the phone. "I think this is going to take me a minute. Why don't you look through this?"

Surprise hit Terra as Alex held his wallet out to her. Reluctantly, she took it. "Are you sure?" she asked, holding the folded leather. It didn't feel right digging through his wallet.

"Mmm," he answered as he scrolled through the missed calls and messages on his phone.

Terra glanced at the screen. Someone was really trying to get ahold of him. There were a lot of missed calls. Turning her attention back to the wallet, she looked at it, considering her options. *Why the hell not?* He'd given it to her for just that reason.

Flipping the leather open, she searched in it and found his driver's license tucked into a slot in the front. A card stuck to the back as she pulled the thin plastic free. It fluttered to the table and landed faced down. Terra set the wallet down and picked up the fallen card. On the front was the same symbol from Alex's bag and a number, but nothing else. Setting it on the wallet, Terra turned to study Alex's ID.

Alexander Fied. Born 1856. *Holy hell! The man was*

over a hundred and fifty years old! Terra sat, shocked by the information. There was no way that could be true. He didn't seem anywhere near that old.

"Mmm."

The noise that came out of Alex shook Terra out of her shock. He reached over and carefully took his ID out of her fingers. "Alexander Fied." The tone of his voice told Terra that he accepted this information as his.

"I told you I was at least as old as that woman." He turned the card so Terra could see it again. "Well, at least we have a place to start." He picked up the card on his wallet and stared at it for a moment before tucking both it and the identification back into the billfold. Pulling out a ten, he dropped it on the table and stuck everything back into the pockets of the jacket. "Come on."

Terra looked up when he patted her on the leg and slid from the booth. She watched him stand up and slip into the soft leather jacket. It settled around him like it was supposed to be there. Yes. She may not know much about the man, but that was definitely his coat. Dread crept into her heart as she slid from the booth.

"So, what now?" she asked, not knowing if she wanted the answer. Terra wanted to smack him when he made another one of those contemplative noises. Didn't the man know how to give a proper answer?

Alex led her through a door in the corner and up a ramp. "I need to find out what happened yesterday," he finally answered.

A sigh slipped from Terra. *Of course, he needed to find*

out what had happened. And now that they had found out who he was, he didn't need her help anymore.

"Well then, if you don't need me anymore, I'll just…" her words trailed off. She couldn't finish that sentence. If she left now, she knew she would never see him again. The men that had broken into her house were only a passing thought compared to the heart-deep pain she was feeling. How could she have grown so attached to this man in the very short time she had known him?

"No," Alex said as he wrapped his arm around her shoulders and pulled her into his side. "You can't leave yet. It's not safe for you to go home."

A mix of emotions washed the pain away. It was nice that he thought about her safety, but it was disappointing that that was his only protest. *Had that tea brought him to his senses about the whole mating thing?* She shook off that thought and shifted away from him. She needed to get a grip on herself. Obviously, Alex had a job to do, and she needed to let him do it.

"Go do what you need to. I'll…" She paused as she thought about her choices. "…wait here." It was the only idea that fit. She couldn't go home yet, but she didn't really have anywhere else to go.

Alex chuckled and pulled her back into his side. "No," he said as they turned a corner and stepped into what looked like a locker room. "I need you safe." He stopped and moved her around so she was facing him.

"And this place isn't safe?" she asked, worried. Glancing around, she searched for possible dangers.

There wasn't anything unusual. A soft laugh rumbled up between them.

"I'm not sure." Alex tilted his head as if he were thinking hard. "Something isn't sitting right with me, but I can't identify it." He looked back into her eyes. There was a heat there that set Terra on fire. "And I'm not about to risk it." Sliding his hand up to her head, he weaved his fingers into her hair and leaned in. The kiss he laid on her lips was hot, passionate, and possessive.

Terra moaned lightly as he pulled her closer and deepened the embrace. Her hands slipped up inside his coat as he held her. If she had any doubts about his feelings before, this burnt them up.

After a few moments, he pulled back reluctantly. He took several short breaths before pulling her in to rest her cheek on his chest.

Terra held on for dear life as she waited for the tingling racing through her body to subside.

"I will not take chances with you." The words rumbled from his chest. Had Terra not been leaning against him, she might not have caught them. After a few more minutes, he pushed her back so she was standing on her own. "Come with me." Taking her hand, he led her deeper into the room.

Three rows of lockers stood with benches between them. Alex stopped at the end of one of the rows and turned to face a locker. He jiggled the handle on the thing, but the door was stuck tight. Terra grinned when he made another one of those contemplative noises and reached up and banged on the top corner of the door. The door swung free, revealing a whole world of things.

Alex grinned as he reached in and started pulling stuff out. "Shoes." He lifted a pair of heavy boots from the bottom of the locker. "Oh, how I've missed you!" Stepping back, he sat down on the bench and slipped his feet out of the slippers Terra had gotten him.

Terra glanced in the locker, eager to find out what it could tell her about Alex. The inside of the door was covered in photos. Most of them were men or dragons. She scanned the faces. Several of them were repeated in the photos as their owners posed together. Alex was in many, but he was always the one standing on the edge of the group. She glanced back at him as he settled his feet into his boots. *He* was *the standoffish type.* She looked at the photos again. Not a single one of them was of Alex and what could be a girlfriend. *A hundred and fifty years old, and the man didn't have a girlfriend. That was kind of sad.*

"That is *so* much better."

Terra turned as Alex stood up and picked the slippers up.

He tucked them into the bottom of the locker and slipped his coat off. Holding the jacket out, he turned to Terra. "Here." He shifted it around so she could put it on.

"What?" Terra looked at the coat, confused.

"Put this on," Alex said as he wrapped the soft leather around Terra's shoulders. "You'll need it." He made Terra slip her arms down the sleeves so it was on properly.

"Why?" she asked. The smooth leather jacket had a thick lining. It would be nice outside, but the temperature in the building was almost too warm for it. Especially with the heat Alex's body had left in it. *Mmm, it smelled like him, too.*

"Trust me." Alex turned back to the locker and pulled a black motorcycle helmet from the shelf at the top. "You are going to want it in a minute." Turning, he slammed the locker door shut and led the way to another door. "Come on, I have something I need to check out."

Terra stood there and considered her dragon man for a moment. Ever since he had gotten his memories back, he had become cryptic. And Terra wasn't sure she liked that very much. "Where are we going?" she asked as she moved over to him.

Alex let out a deep breath before answering. "There was something I was supposed to do yesterday, and I need to find out if I did it."

"Check on Melanie?" Terra asked.

Alex nodded and ushered her out into the main barn. "Yes." He sounded grim. "I don't think things went very well, but I have to go find out."

Terra nodded. If there were something he needed to do, she would help however she could. Turning her attention to the large room, she looked around. There wasn't much going on here. A few racks of things sat along one wall, but most of the space was empty. A large door hung open on one side of the room. Alex's gentle hand on her back guided her into the room and pointed her to the corner where a lone motorcycle sat by itself. It could have been a Harley, but Terra wasn't sure.

"Come on," Alex said again, ushering her across the

room. Stopping next to the bike, he turned and slipped the helmet onto Terra's head. "You probably won't need this, but…" he let his words go without finishing.

Terra smiled as he worked the strap tight under her chin. "You know, we could take my car," she offered.

"True." Alex grinned as he went to the motorcycle and started it up. "But then I wouldn't have an excuse to keep you close." He held out his hand for Terra.

Taking his hand, Terra climbed on the bike behind him. Soon, Alex had the bike out the door and was tooling down the road as Terra held on to him. She rested her head against his back to better enjoy the ride. God, she hoped he knew where he was going.

THE WIND that had been pulling the warmth from the leather jacket slowed as Alex turned down a dirt road. Terra sat up more as Alex guided the bike between the deep grooves of the path. It was a good thing they hadn't brought her car. It would have never survived the trip over the rutted-up road. As it was, Alex had to take it easy, or the uneven ground would bounce them both off the bike. Terra gritted her teeth and clung to Alex's warm back as they went.

About a half a mile of hard riding brought them to a tall farmhouse. The building was well maintained and looked quite pleasant. Alex stopped the bike in front of the building but didn't turn it off.

Terra waited as he watched the front of the house. Tired of being on the bike, she shifted so she could get up and stretch the cramps out of her back and legs. Unused to sitting in that position for so long, she was ready to get off the bike for a while.

Alex's hand came down on her leg, stopping her from getting up. "Not here," he said softly and kicked off, setting the bike back in motion.

Confused, Terra turned to look at the quiet farmhouse. Movement from one of the curtains caught her attention. "Someone's there," she yelled over the sound of the bike.

"I know," Alex called back, "but it isn't who we're looking for."

"How do you know?" she yelled back. Hadn't they just traveled a long way over rough roads to find out what had happened yesterday?

Alex sat quietly for a moment as he guided the bike back down the dirt road. "The window was broken."

Okay… Confusion welled up inside of Terra. *What difference does a broken window make?* "Explain," she called.

Shaking his head, Alex took a long, deep breath before answering. "I can't. My instincts tell me something's wrong, and I'm not about to take any chances at the moment. Give me a little time, and I'll figure something out. "

Nodding, Terra turned her head and leaned her cheek against Alex's back. It must be bothersome to have your instincts lead you around like that. But then again, if his instincts had just saved them from some unknown danger, maybe they weren't all bad.

TERRA WAS MORE than ready to get off the bike when Alex finally pulled into the drive of a ranch-style home. "Can I get down now?" she asked.

A soft chuckle slipped from Alex as he held the motorcycle up. "Yes," he said, amused.

Climbing off the bike, Terra pulled her helmet off and looked at this house. It was a really nice house. The outside was wrapped in brown clapboard siding and edged with river rocks. The huge yard was elegantly landscaped and well maintained. *Very impressive.* "So who lives here?"

Alex let out another soft laugh. "I do." Having set the bike on its kickstand, he went up to the double-car garage and pushed one of the rolling doors up.

"Oh!" Terra said, feeling foolish. She propped the helmet on the back seat of the bike and followed Alex into the garage. "It's very nice." She paused to look around the man's garage. It was very neatly organized. A dark green SUV took up one side of the spacious garage.

"Thank you," he said as he unlocked the inside door. "It's home." He held the door open so Terra could enter.

Hurrying along, she stepped through the door and onto a rosy, wooden floor. She looked around for a second before heading down the short hall towards a living room. The place was nicely done in dark tones with wood accents. Terra paused just past a set of steps and glanced around the open floor plan. The room was very spacious. A comfy-looking couch face a large, stone fireplace on her right, while an amazing kitchen sprawled out to her left. The two areas were separated with a bar-height counter made of the same river stone as the fireplace.

Placing his hand on her lower back, Alex slipped past Terra into the kitchen space.

She stepped forwards out of his way before following him into the kitchen. "So, you got your memories back?"

Alex made an annoyed sound deep in his chest. "Mostly," he answered as he pulled open the refrigerator.

Terra made a matching annoyed sound. Before they had stopped at The Dragon's Wing, he had talked in complete sentences. Now that he was regaining his memories, he was being cryptic, and she didn't like that one bit.

Alex must have felt or heard Terra's irritation. He let out a deep sigh and shut the refrigerator door. "Yes, I have regained most of my memories." He came over and took up Terra's hands. "But there are still things I can't remember. Important things." Lifting her hands up, he laid a kiss on the back of them before holding them to his chest. "I just need a little more time to sort through the stuff in my head before I can decide what to do." He shifted both of her hands to one of his and reached out to push a stray lock of hair away from her face. "Please, have a little patience with me as I work through this."

Terra felt like a heel. Here she was, irritated that he wasn't sharing his thoughts when he was still sorting through them. Of course it would take a little time to sift through a lifetime of memories. And it would be irritating that there were important pieces missing.

"I'm sorry." She dropped her eyes away from his as she apologized. "I didn't mean to push you."

Reaching out, Alex pulled her in against him. "It's all right," he reassured her as he rested his cheek against her hair. "I haven't been very attentive." Wrapping his arms around her, he held Terra close.

A soft laugh slipped from her as she slid her arms up around his back and rested her head against him. "And I haven't been very patient." She sighed.

"It's all right." His voice held a hint of contentment. "Today hasn't been easy on either of us." He held her for a while longer before letting out a long sigh and loosening his hold on her. "Why don't you make yourself at home, and I'll make us something to eat?"

Terra smiled at him. "That sounds like a wonderful idea." It had been several hours since they'd had breakfast.

They stood together for a moment longer before Alex pulled away. He placed a light kiss on Terra's cheek before releasing her completely. "Is there anything special you would like?" he asked as he went back and opened the refrigerator.

"Whatever." Terra shrugged and shifted uncomfortably. The morning had been long, and that ride on the bike hadn't done her any good. "Can I borrow your bathroom?"

"It's around the corner, under the steps." Alex nodded back to the short hall that led to the garage.

It took Terra a moment to find the half bath tucked

under the stairs. The wall was lined with knotty pine panels, and the door blended right in. Had it not been for the small loop handle, she would never have seen it. It was a very nice way to tuck the washroom out of the way. Pulling off Alex's coat, she folded it over the sink and dropped the leather bag on the floor. She was actually surprised to find the thing still on her hip. It wasn't very heavy, and she had totally forgotten that she had it.

Sitting down, she relaxed and let her mind wander over the morning. They had finally figured out who her mystery man was. Alexander Fied. A dragon with a job to do. And a very nice house. Terra glanced around the small room. It was painted the same rich browns as the rest of the house. *And to think, he was worried about not having anything to offer a mate.*

That thought gave her a moment's pause. *A dragon's mate. What did that really mean?* The way Alex had talked about it, Terra was sure it was something permanent, like marriage. Surprisingly, that idea didn't scare Terra much. She hadn't known him very long, but Alex seemed like the type of person her mother would approve of. Of course, they would have to start out by dating for a while first. Jumping straight into any relationship was a stupid idea, but she could see potential in the man. *Alexander Fied. Eww.* If she did stay with him, she would have to seriously think about taking his name. That would make her Terra Fied. Terrified. Yeah, that wasn't going to happen.

And how would it work out, anyway? If the information she had learned was correct, dragons lived for hundreds of years. Alex's own identification listed him as over one hundred and fifty years old, though he looked nowhere near that age. But what about her? She would only live to be eighty or ninety. And she would age, while he would not. Yeah, that wasn't going to work in a relationship no matter how much you cared for someone. Terra drew in a deep breath and made her decision. It didn't matter how much she liked the man or how good their chemistry was, they could never have a future together. Maybe a few good years until she started to age, but then what? No, it was better to let him go now before things got out of control.

Finishing her business, Terra washed her hands and glanced at herself in the mirror. The vision that greeted her was horrifying. Being shoved under a helmet hadn't done anything for her hair. Digging in her bag, she pulled out a brush and set about doing something with the mess on her head. Once it was back in place, she dropped the brush back into her purse, slipped the strap of the leather bag back over her head, and pulled on Alex's jacket so she didn't have to carry it. When she returned to the kitchen, she would give him back his things and explain that she couldn't be his mate. Terra gave herself one last nod in the mirror and opened the door to go face her dragon man.

Terra squeaked in surprise as a hand came out from behind her and covered her mouth. Something sharp bit into the skin of her neck, and heat flowed from that point as her assailant injected her with some unknown substance. Adrenaline raced into Terra's system as she realized what was happening. She had just been drugged! Remembering her self-defense classes, she went limp in her attacker's grasp. The hand covering her mouth slipped away as she dropped unexpectedly. *"Alex!"* she screamed as she twisted, driving an elbow into the body behind her.

Apparently, the man attacking her hadn't expected her to fight back. He grunted as the well-placed hit drove the air from his lungs.

Terra scrambled away before he could regain his grasp on her. The sound of running boots on the hard-wood floor gave her hope. She found a place against the wall and reached up to the needle still stuck in her neck. Pulling it out, Terra covered the wound with her free hand. Whatever had been in the hypodermic was burning its way along her veins. She turned and watched as Alex came down on her attacker like a fury from hell. The edge of her vision wavered, and she tilted her head up, trying to stop the slow spin the world had acquired. It didn't help. Terra closed her eyes as the sound of the struggles subsided. Hopefully, Alex had beaten the crap out of that guy and would know what to do for her. She was in no shape to make any decisions at the moment.

AFTER DIRECTING Terra to the bathroom, Alex turned back to the refrigerator and pulled the door open. There had to be something in there good enough to eat. He wrinkled his nose at the contents. *Leftovers and lunchmeats.* True, he wasn't a bad cook, but his dragon refused to let him offer her anything but the best, and these scraps were far from his best. Deciding on the lunchmeat, he pulled out two packs of cold cuts and some cheese. He dropped them on the counter and went to the pantry to get a fresh tomato. What he found there horrified him. One of the tomatoes had gone bad while he was gone. There was no way he was going to serve that to his mate!

When that thought hit him, he stopped, staring at the contents of his cupboard without seeing them. He had to stop that train of thought right there. Yes, Terra did have the potential to be his mate, but there was no way he could offer her that right now. Regaining his memories had been both a blessing and a curse. Yes, he was in a position to offer her a comfortable life, but he also had a very stressful job that took up a lot of his time. He was an Elite in Eternity. A job that few could do. And with someone killing dragons, his skills would be in more demand than ever. There was no way he would be able to hold down a healthy relationship while trying to help investigate the murdered dragons.

Letting out a deep sigh, Alex picked the basket of tomatoes up and looked at the ruined fruit. He pulled the bad one out and dropped it into the waste can. The remaining tomatoes looked all right. They just needed a good washing. Moving the basket to the sink, he set about cleaning them as he thought.

Why did life have to present a mate right now? Why couldn't it have been six months ago, before the whole issue with the solitary dragons list started? Then he could have quit Eternity and set about courting his mate properly. No one would have even questioned him for giving up his job. All of the men he had gone through training with were already retired. The only person who had been in the service longer was Daniel, and he was the king's right-hand man.

Over the last few years, Alex had been drifting away from the men he worked with. Their social gatherings didn't appeal to him as much as they had in the past. He just didn't feel any real connection with the younger crowd rising up through the ranks. Hell, if it hadn't been for his job, he would probably be on the solitary dragons list already.

That thought stopped Alex. *The solitary dragons list.* All of the missing people had been on that list. Stepping back into motion, Alex moved the tomatoes to a cutting board and started to slice them up for sandwiches. His thoughts churned over everything he had learned about the list of victims he'd been given. Other than being on the list, there wasn't much they had in common. They ranged in age between just over a hundred to just under five hundred. Their backgrounds were different. Their habits were different. Their dragon types were different. There were both males and females. It boggled Alex's mind as he tried to figure out what they all had in common. Just that blasted list.

Alex paused again as another thought struck him. *Maybe that was the connection. They had all been on that list.* He worked his battered memories to see what he could recall of the records of old dragons. It took a moment, but something else occurred to Alex. There were actually two lists of solitary dragons—those under five hundred and those over five hundred. The older dragons had lived in a time when it was dangerous to be dragons and preferred to remain hidden away from the world. For their peace of mind, only the highest level of Eternity had access to that list, but Alex was sure he would have heard if one of the ancient dragons had been killed.

There hadn't been any noticeable increase in disappearances of dragons under one hundred. But these dragons weren't tracked as closely as the older dragons were. In fact, it was rather hard to tell the difference between a dragon and a human unless someone told you. Everything fell into place as Alex moved on to cutting up the cheese. The individuals who had disappeared had been targeted *because* they had been on the solitary dragons list. *That made sense!* Working off the list was the only way to ensure that the people you were going after really were dragons. The answer had been staring them in the face the entire time, and everyone had missed it. Now he just had to figure out how that list had gotten into the hands of the group responsible for the murders.

A squeak from the hall drew Alex out of his thoughts. He looked up from the counter just as Terra screamed his name. Dropping the half-made sandwich, he bolted from the kitchen and skidded into the hall. Rage coursed through his veins when he saw Terra stumble away from a man. *Mine!* Red filled his vision as he and his dragon roared in anger. The distance to the intruder disappeared as he barreled into the man, knocking him back into the wall. Two quick punches had the man down. A few more made sure he wasn't going to get up anytime soon.

Alex stepped back and looked at the unconscious man. His dragon wanted to tear the intruder limb from limb, but Alex wanted him alive to find out who he was and why he was there. Pushing down the rage, Alex turned around. There were more important things to take care of at the moment.

Chapter 11

"Terra?" Alex spoke her name softly as he went to where she was leaning against the wall. She didn't look good at all. A trickle of blood ran down the side of her neck from some kind of wound hidden under her hand. Her fair skin was flushed, and she was starting to break a sweat. "Terra?" he called her name again as he reached for her. Pulling her hand away from her neck, he checked on the wound. It was only a small tear, and it had almost stopped bleeding already. He pressed his thumb over the wound to apply the pressure it needed to seal.

The steady pressure drew Terra out of whatever haze she was in. She tried to focus on him, but Alex could see there was something wrong with her. Both of her pupils were blown up huge. Something clattered to the floor next to them.

Alex glanced down at the hypodermic needle that had fallen from her hand. His eyes came back up to her.

Worry quickened his pulse. "Terra?" he said again as he pulled her into his arms. Her assailant had to have dosed her with some kind of drug, but the question was, with what?

"Alex," she finally answered as she shifted to lean against him.

A whiff of scent hit him, driving his dragon to near frenzy. He knew this scent, but it shouldn't have been coming from her. *Dragon hormones.* And not the ones that had been making the rounds in the clubs. These were the hormones put out by a female dragon at the peak of her fertile cycle. It was one of the few things that could drive a male dragon out of his mind. His body tightened with need. This was not going to be pleasant for either of them. "Come on." Clamping down on his control, he tried to ignore the physical reaction he was having to the pheromones coming off her. They needed help. Badly. There was no telling what else had been in that needle.

Wrapping his arm around her back, Alex shifted Terra to his side to help her to the garage door. He opened it and slammed it shut again. There were two more men in the garage. He clicked the lock into place and looked back at the man he had knocked out. No wonder he'd gone down so easily—he had been cannon fodder, sent in to dose Terra. Then, when the pheromones bouncing around in her system affected Alex, his buddies would come in and finish the job. *Who the hell* were *these people?*

"Come on." Alex coaxed Terra back towards the living room. Since the garage was blocked, they had to find another way out. The back door should provide a good exit. The sound of breaking glass stopped him. Of course, whoever these people were would have the back of his house guarded as well. *Crap.*

For half a second, Alex considered taking Terra upstairs, but that would corner them. That was a bad idea. Pushing that thought away, he turned back to the small hall leading to the garage. "This way."

Terra nodded and followed his direction.

Running his fingers over the knotty pine paneling next to the bathroom, Alex found the seam he was looking for. Digging his nails into the crack, he pulled open the hidden utility closet. Until a few weeks ago, this space had held his ageing water heater. Alex had pulled the damned thing out when it had sprung a leak and ruined part of the wall in his closet. Instead of replacing the damaged appliance with a new one, Alex had decided to go with one of those inline water heaters, leaving the utility cabinet empty.

"Get in." Alex pushed Terra towards the dark closet.

She nodded again and climbed inside without question.

Aww hell. Terra's unquestioning response set all of Alex's instincts tingling. He had never seen the new designer drug in action, but he'd read all the reports on how it affected its victims. They would start out delirious and move on to highly suggestible. That described Terra's condition perfectly. Alex pushed her farther into the closet and climbed in behind her. Pulling the door closed, he ran through the list of symptoms, hoping he wasn't right.

Working around her, Alex reached for the wall at the

back of the closet. Terra let out a soft moan, confirming Alex's fears. On top of the female hormones, she seemed to have been dosed with the drug making the rounds in the clubs. The next phase would find her insatiable and demanding. This was the reason getting a rape charge out in court was so hard. You couldn't really call it rape when the woman was the aggressor. Even if she were being driven by a chemical reaction. They needed to get out of there now. He was barely holding out against the pheromones as it was. It was going to be even harder when they started affecting her. Alex shushed her softly and popped the piece of drywall out of the wall. He'd been working on patching the damaged wall for a while now, but everything had blown up at work, and he hadn't found time to finish nailing the new board in place. Now he was glad he hadn't.

The new opening led into the back corner of Alex's closet. Sliding the plaster out of the way, Alex guided Terra out into the open space he had made to work. She moaned again as his hands touched her. It was not going to be long now before she completely lost control.

Sliding the closet door open, Alex looked out into his bedroom. So far, there was no one there. "Come on." He pushed Terra out into the open space next to his bed. If he could just get her outside, he had a plan that might work to get them away. His hand slid down to the small of her back, driving a much louder moan from her. There was no way they were going to make it out if she continued to make sounds like that. He was going to have to do something fast before the intruders heard her.

Grabbing her in his arms, Alex turned Terra around and dropped his lips to hers. A zing of lust washed through him, driving all thought from his brain. He was already hard with desire, but the taste of her lips drove him to the very edge of his control. He groaned as he pulled her in against him. Her arms came around him, and she pressed into his front eagerly. The feel of her against him was exquisite. All thought of the men invading his home ran from his mind, and they stood together, lost in each other's passion.

A rustle of scales broke through the lust as the sounds of footsteps on the stairs echoed through the room. *Danger to Mine!* his dragon growled, reminding him of their situation. They needed to get out of there. He pulled himself away from Terra's clutching hands just enough so he could think again.

Sliding his hands to her hips, Alex pressed Terra back without releasing her lips. If he could just move them to the other end of the room, he had a plan for their escape. Slowly, he walked her backwards across the room. The hungry sounds she was making were muffled in his mouth. A note of hope crept into his heart as he continued to kiss and guide her towards the far wall. Stepping on the heels of his boots, he worked them off as they went.

As the passion rose between them, Terra started tugging at his shirt.

He moved so she could work his shirt up his back. Alex drew in a gasp of air as her nails scraped over his skin in her haste to get him out of his clothing, but the rumbled warning from his dragon helped him resist the urge to pull her against him again.

Their lips parted long enough for Terra to rip the shirt up and over his head. The cool air on his hot skin made him suck in more air. The thought of danger gave him the strength he needed to resist giving in to his urges.

She threw the cloth to the floor and returned to his mouth with more vigor than before. Her tongue worked against his with a passion that tested Alex to his limits. He moaned as her hands dropped to the waistband of his pants and yanked on the button, ripping it open.

Catching her wrists, he stopped her before she could slide her hand down inside his clothing. If her delicate fingers worked against his hardened length, even the warning his dragon was screaming at him wouldn't be enough to get them out of there. He was barely hanging on as it was. Lifting her hands away from their goal, he wrapped them around his back and pulled her against him again. Her clothing was coarse against his oversensitive skin, but he held her to him, trying to keep her moving backwards to the far wall. If he just concentrated on reaching that wall, he could push back the desire racing through him.

She made another desperate noise that he caught in his mouth. Her nails bit into the skin of his back, fraying his control even more. Had she been any other woman, he might have given in at that moment. But she was his mate—*Mine!*—and he had to keep her safe. That one instinct was the only thing counteracting the hormones racing through his system. Giving in to the overwhelming need flowing through them both would only get them caught. Breaking their kiss, Alex glanced behind Terra to see how far they had to go. There were only a few feet left.

Denied access to his mouth, Terra moaned and dropped her lips to Alex's collarbone.

He groaned as she kissed and nibbled her way down his clavicle. Tilting his head back to give her better access, he moved her those last few steps to the wall. A soft growl rumbled up from his chest as he bent back to her and reclaimed her lips. He kissed her passionately as he pressed his body over hers, pinning her to the wall. She groaned again as he shifted back and pushed the rest of his clothing over his hips. They slid to the floor with a soft thump.

Her fingers ghosted over his back, heading for the newly exposed skin.

Alex caught her hands before they could reach below his waist. Lacing their fingers together, he lifted their hands up over Terra's head. He pressed his hip into her, unable to resist the pull of his desire. She was warm and solid under him. His crumbling willpower was starting to collapse, but his dragon forced him to hold on to the scattered shreds.

She moaned again and squirmed with desire.

Gasping for breath, he pulled away from her lips. If he didn't stop this right now, he would be lost to the passion that had risen between them. Staring down into her eyes, he tried to get a grip on himself. The sight that met him drove him to the very edge.

She was gorgeous. A light sheen of sweat made her

skin glisten as she panted in need. The blue of her eyes had darkened in passion, and the widening of the pupils made them impossibly deep. Alex would have given nearly anything to stare into those desire-filled eyes for all eternity.

Now is not the time, his dragon growled at him. *There will be a time, and soon.*

Alex had to shake himself to break the effect she had on him. He kissed her softly, pulling away before she could devour his lips again. "It's time to be quiet," he warned as he shifted away from her slightly. He needed as much of his mind as he could gather to plan their escape.

Terra growled her displeasure and leaned into him, placing kisses on the skin she could reach. Shivers of desire raced through Alex, but he pushed them away. When they were safe again, he would take the time to explore the passion that had built between them. Right now, he had things to do. He caught her mouth for one last, hard kiss before getting to work.

Separating her hands, he bent them down behind her and pulled her against his body again. A shiver racked her frame as he held her tightly to him. Turning his attention away from the wanton woman in his arms, he glanced out the glass door that led to the patio. The blinds were turned so no one could see in, but he could make out the shape of a man standing on his back porch.

Alex inched them closer to the door as he weighed his options. One man he could handle. He could rush the guy and take him down with ease. But, that would mean that he would have to turn Terra loose. And with the way she was nibbling on his collarbone, that wasn't something he was willing to do. Besides, there was no telling how many other people were lurking around his home.

"They're gone!" a voice yelled from inside the house. "Get in here and help us find them!"

Alex's heart soared as the man on the back porch went in through the other glass door. *Perfect.* With the man inside, he had a chance to make an escape, but he was going to have to do it fast. If the intruders were searching the house, it would only make sense that they would start with the rooms closest to where they entered. The master bedroom would be the first door on the right.

Just as Alex feared, the handle on his door jiggled. Grabbing up Terra, he bolted to the glass door and slammed the thing open.

Terra gasped in pain as he bent her arms too far in his haste.

"Hold on, love," Alex hissed as he loosened his grasp so her arms weren't twisted at such an odd angle. Racing down the steps, he took two strides across the stone patio before releasing his hold on his dragon. Scales burst out as he shifted into his grand form. Terra screamed in fear, but he ignored her protests as he grasped her tightly in his claws and beat his wings down.

The sound of two shots rang out. The bullets stung as they ricocheted off his scaled hide. He had shifted just in time to prevent major injury, but it still hurt like hell. Letting out a roar, Alex flapped harder, trying to gain altitude. His grand dragon form was large, but he wasn't used to carrying the weight of another person... even if she was small.

Alex clutched Terra to him as he aimed for the woods lining the back edge of his property. If he just skimmed the tops of the trees, he could cover a fair distance without his attackers being able to track him.

The tip of Terra's nails dug into his scales as he flew, but he didn't stop. The feel of the shivers racing down her body almost made him change his mind. She had to be terrified. Clinging to the underside of a dragon that was skimming along the upper branches of a forest couldn't be very pleasant. Alex added a few more feet of height so she wouldn't hit the topmost branches. The feel of Terra's fingers gripping his scales eased a little, but her shivering didn't subside. The need to find a place to land ate at him. He had to find out what was wrong with her. *Could one of the stray bullets have hit her?*

A jolt of fear raced through Alex, and he scanned the area for a safe place to land, but there was nothing close. He followed his instincts as they pushed him to the right. He may be missing some of his memories, but he still trusted his dragon to keep him safe.

THE SIGHT of an opening in the forest relieved some of the anxiety filling Alex. Terra's shivers had stopped, but so had the feel of her nails digging into his scales. He had to set down here no matter what. During his flight, there had been several breaks in the canopy, but none of the clearings had been safe for him to land in. They were either too small or had signs of people. With Terra being drugged and possibly hurt, he didn't want to risk an encounter with an unknown person.

Alex landed in the open field and looked around. *Perfect.* He even knew where they were. A large, grassy lawn led up to a small cabin set at the very edge of the woods—one of the many rest spots Eternity kept for their traveling agents! Of course his dragon would lead him to a place where they would be safe.

Laying Terra on the soft grass, Alex backed up to look her over. She was unnervingly still. Nuzzling her softly, he drew in a deep breath. The air was free of the tang of blood, but it was filled with a heady concoction of pheromones.

Terra moaned softly as Alex's snout bumped into her stomach.

Pulling his head back, Alex shook it, trying to clear his mind. He sat down on the grass to think. Terra was alive, but she was also out cold. It had to have been a mixture of the hormones in her system and the adrenaline from their flight. Well, at least now he wasn't going to have to fight against her reaction to the drugs.

Looking down at her still form, he studied her. *Mine!* His dragon's declaration rattled through him so hard it made his teeth clench. *That could be an issue.* He cocked his head to get a better look at Terra. Warmth and contentment swirled up through him. He let out a deep sigh and shifted back to his human form. There was no fighting it now. Sometime during their harrowing escape, his dragon had laid claim to the woman. A true bonding wouldn't be complete until he shared a scale with her, but no matter what he did, he belonged to her now.

Bending down, Alex scooped Terra up and headed towards the little cabin. He laughed softly as he stepped onto the covered porch. This was his cabin. Well, it wasn't exactly *his* cabin, but it was the one he took care of. Eternity kept a series of small houses across the country, places where their agents could stop and rest as they went about their business. They were free to be used at any time by any agent. The agent was just expected to leave the place the way they found it. There was a special monitoring system that would alert the main office when one of the houses was in use, and they, in turn, would alert the keeper of the house that the building was in use and when the occupant left so it could be checked. It was a very convenient system. And a lot cheaper than constantly paying for hotel rooms.

Alex dropped Terra's feet to the floor and held her against him as he punched in his code to unlock the key box. Each agent had their own code that would be reported back to the main office. Taking the key, Alex opened the door and carried Terra inside. The cabin was just the way he'd left it on his last inspection—nice and clean.

Crossing the one-roomed cabin, Alex set Terra on the double bed. Carefully, he shifted her around, undressing her. She wouldn't need his coat or that stupid bag. He paused to look at it. A piece that he had been missing slipped back into place. *The bag!* He dropped the satchel to the floor and turned back to Terra. His revelation could wait until he had seen her put to bed properly.

Leaving her in just her T-shirt and underwear, he paused to admire her. This was the view he had missed this morning when she had gotten up to shower. He'd been a fool not to appreciate it then. Carefully, he pushed her slightly rumpled hair back from her face as she relaxed in his arms. He wanted to kiss her and hold her against him. To feel her soft flesh against his again. That had been an amazing way to wake up. It would be an even more amazing way to go to sleep. Of course, there were some very vigorous activities he would like to do with her between the time of going to bed and falling asleep, but that would have to wait until later. He still had things to do, and she was in no condition for what he had in mind. Shaking the image away, he pulled her up and tucked her in under the covers.

"Get some rest, love," he whispered.

Placing a light kiss on her forehead, he stood up and away from her. That was all he was going to allow himself to do until he was sure the pheromones were out of her system. He wanted to make sure their first time together was something special, not rutting driven by a chemical reaction. And definitely not when she was unconscious!

It took him a moment, but he pushed back the thoughts of his mate and turned his mind to what had to be done next. There were still questions he needed to answer. One thing that boggled his mind was the group that was kidnapping dragons. How had they found his home? He was sure he hadn't been followed from Melanie's house, but they had showed up awfully quickly after he and Terra had arrived at his place. Could their attackers have been waiting for them? And if so, how would they even know where he lived? That bothered Alex.

Picking up his leather bag, he took it to the dinette table. It was surprising that Terra had still been carrying the thing—he had forgotten all about it. *How could I have forgotten about something so important?* He laughed at himself. That was the stupidest thing he could have possibly thought after the last two days. He had forgotten most of his life. Of course he could forget about something as small as a bag. No matter how important it was.

Dumping the bag out on table, Alex sifted through its contents. The fact that Terra had added her things to it made him smile. He moved her purse to the side and considered his things. There was the file, a pack of gum, and the silver necklace. Moving the file and gum back to the bag, he considered the necklace. That was the important thing he had forgotten. He couldn't quite remember how he'd gotten it, but he knew it had something to do with the men chasing him.

He stared at the charm for a long time, trying to remember how he'd acquired it. The memory played with the back of his mind, but he just couldn't get it to come out. The only things he was sure about were that he'd gotten it when he went to check on Melanie, and that the last of his missing dragons was dead. Just like the rest of the dragons in his file.

Reaching out, Alex touched the charm. The sting of magic bit his fingers, but he didn't pull back. This was why the mystery group was after him, and he needed to find out what it was. Clenching his teeth against the pain, he pressed his hand down over the charm. The longer he touched the metal, the more the energy radiated up his arm. When the pain got too much to handle, Alex pulled his hand away. He could feel his dragon half writhing in agony, as if the magic had tried to tear it out of him. As the power faded, Alex could feel a distance between his two halves—something he had never known. It was weird. Slowly, the sensation subsided, leaving him whole again.

Someone needs to know about this, but who?

Alex turned away from the charm and went to get his phone out of the pocket of his coat. There were fifteen missed calls and as many text messages. And that was just since they had left The Dragon's Wing. Who the hell could have wanted to get a hold of him so badly? Alex scrolled through the log. Most of the calls and texts had come from one number. Sanders.

Sanders liked to keep a line on the agents under him, but Alex couldn't remember him ever being this fussy about someone not checking in. Then again, he had never gone missing before. Plus, there had been that whole business with Michael. He had only been missing for a few days before turning back up with Lady Carissa. What a fiasco that had been! The poor man was still on medical leave as he learned to live with his new instincts.

And being bonded to the king's sister probably didn't make his life any easier.

Alex shook his head as he thought. He couldn't imagine what Michael was going through. To suddenly have instincts pushing one around would be rather unsettling, but then again, Alex relied on his other half to keep him out of trouble. Most of the time, his dragon made better decisions than he did. Alex glanced over at Terra, asleep on the bed. Hopefully, his instincts had made a better decision than his rational mind when it came to her. Only time would tell.

Letting out a long breath, Alex turned his thoughts back to his phone and the man who had blown it up. Maybe Sanders did have cause to worry, but did he have to disturb everyone in his search for Alex? Brigs had mentioned that the man had blown up everyone's phones looking for his missing man. Alex held his finger over the call log, ready to return the worried man's call, but a growl from his dragon stopped him from placing it. Sanders' worry was way out of proportion for the situation. That didn't sit right with Alex. Shifting his finger down, Alex called the number that appeared in the call log only once.

"Hello." Daniel's voice rolled out of the phone.

"I need to talk with you," Alex said, getting straight to the point.

There was a long pause before Daniel answered him. "Is everything all right, Alex?"

"No," Alex answered. "There is something seriously wrong, and I need to speak with you, alone, as soon as possible."

Daniel let another pregnant pause hold the space between them. "All right. Will you be coming here?"

Alex thought about it for a moment as he listened to his dragon. "No," he said softly. His dragon did not like the idea of going into the main office. Something about that idea raised the hackles on the back of his neck. It was also a fair distance, even by wing, and that would leave Terra unprotected for too long. He didn't like leaving her at all, but he needed to get this taken care of. "Can you meet me at The Dragon's Wing?"

"Give me thirty minutes," Daniel answered and hung up.

Alex let out a relieved sight. He wasn't sure what had his dragon so up in arms about going back to the main office, but Daniel should be able to help him put things together. Turning to look at Terra, Alex made his decision. He would leave her here. It would be best to let her rest until the hormones were out of her system.

Pulling her phone out of her purse, he entered his number in her address book. That way, she would be able to contact him in case she woke up before he got back. Dropping the phone on the table with a nice note, Alex gathered his things and slipped them into the bag. For a moment, Alex considered the charm on the table. He didn't want to touch it again, but he needed to take it to Daniel. He needed something he could transport it in—something where he wouldn't have to touch it when handing it off to Daniel. A quick search of the cabinets came up with a plastic sandwich bag. *Perfect.* Using a fork, Alex lifted the necklace up and slipped it into the bag. He dropped the sandwich bag into his satchel.

There. Now he had everything he needed to sort out what had happened to him. One last check on Terra, and he was ready to go. Hopefully, this trip wouldn't take him long, and he could be back well before she woke up.

Chapter 12

"So what's the problem?" Daniel called out as soon as Alex landed.

Alex paused and looked down at the head of Eternity. He hadn't even waited for Alex to shift back to his human form before getting started. Usually, Daniel was more patient than that.

"I need your help with something," Alex answered as he made his way all the way into the barn over The Dragon's Wing.

"I figured that," Daniel said as he crossed his arms over his chest and waited for Alex to come closer. "I've been on the phone all day, trying to sort out whatever you've gotten yourself into. And that's really hard to do when you don't know what the issue is."

"Really?" Alex snorted, amused.

"Yeah," Daniel said. "I can't begin to tell you how many complaints I've received about Sanders today. Apparently, the man has been harassing every agent in this area, looking high and low for you since yesterday. What have you done to ruffle the man's scales so badly?"

Alex snorted out another breath and shifted back to human form. "Other than my job? There's no telling with him," he said as he closed the distance to the head of Eternity. "You know the man worries about everything. And you really shouldn't use that phrase with him. He isn't a dragon."

Brushing off Alex's correction, Daniel let out a deep breath. "In light of recent events, he has good reason to worry. A missing agent is nothing to laugh at. Just ask Michael. Sanders hunted me down last night when you didn't report in. I didn't know what to think."

"That I went home with some hot chick and was too busy to check in?" Alex snarked. As it was, he *had* spent the night with a beautiful woman in his arms, but Daniel didn't need to know that.

Daniel raised an eyebrow at him. "I might believe that from someone else, but not from you. Besides, I hear tell that there was reason to worry. Brigs said a lady brought you in earlier and you seemed a little… off." A note of concern crept into Daniel voice. "Are you all right?"

Alex smiled at him. "See, I told you there was a woman involved," he said as he led the way into the locker room. Letting the sarcasm drop from his voice, he shook his head. "No, I'm not okay." He glanced back to the man following him. "A lot has happened since yesterday."

Daniel followed but didn't press Alex to tell him what had happened. That was one of the things Alex loved about the man. Daniel may ask, but he would sit and wait until you were ready to give up your secrets, even if he were busy.

Drawing in a deep breath, Alex opened up his locker. A wave of things avalanched out of his normally neat space. His eyes opened wide, and he looked up at Daniel. "Something isn't right."

Daniel looked down at the mess spilling across the floor. "I can see that." He paused as he took in the condition of Alex's things. "Why don't you get dressed and then tell me what's happened?"

Nodding, Alex untangled his clothing. Someone had done a very thorough search of his things, and Alex was ready to lay money that they had been looking for the necklace in his bag. But how had they managed to get into The Dragon's Wing and find his locker? Sure, the main barn door was left open so dragons could come and go in their grand forms, but there had to have been forty lockers in here. How did they know which locker was his?

A horrible thought crossed Alex's mind. "How many people have access to the solitary dragons list?" Alex looked up at the shocked expression on Daniel's face. Obviously, the man hadn't been expecting that question.

"Well," Daniel said as he thought, "almost everyone in Eternity has access to some part of the list."

Alex shook his head as he pulled on his shirt. "Not some part. All of it."

Pausing to think, Daniel watched as Alex got dressed. "Only the king and I have access to the full list."

"All right." Alex stood up to face Daniel. "Then who has access to the short list? The one that contains dragons under five hundred years old?"

"What are you playing at, Alex?" Daniel asked.

Alex let out a sigh and pulled the file of missing dragons from his bag. He held it out for Daniel to take. "I've been going through the list of missing dragons, trying to find some connection. Some reason they were taken and others weren't. The only thing they had in common was the solitary dragons list."

Daniel took the folder, opened it, and flipped through the first few pages, glancing over the work Alex had done. "So you think someone targeted these dragons *because* they were on the list?"

"Yes," Alex answered. After much consideration, that was the conclusion he had reached. "I know that different teams are given different parts of the list to work on, and there are only a few of us who have run of the entire list." Reaching out, he tapped the file in Daniel's hands. "These dragons come from different sections of the list. So, either we have one person with access to the master list, or many people leaking their individual sections."

Shock stole across Daniel's face. He closed the file and gave Alex a grim look. "You know what this means?"

"Someone high in Eternity is helping to kill dragons," Alex replied, stating the unthinkable.

The look Daniel gave Alex was skeptical.

Alex held his hands out to the mess that had fallen out of his locker. "How else do you explain this? And there were agents waiting for me when I got home. They attacked Terra—"

A horrible thought hit him. *Terra!* Alex ran his fingers up through his hair, pushing it back from his face. "Oh God! I left Terra at the safe house. Alone!" Grabbing the junk that had fallen out of the locker, he shoved it back in and slammed the door. "I've got to get back!"

"Wait!" Daniel grabbed Alex before he could rush back out. "Which house is she in?"

"Mine." Alex fidgeted as his dragon pushed him to go back to his mate. "The one on Edgewood Drive."

"Come on." Daniel practically dragged Alex into the main room of the pub. "Brigs!" he hollered as he went in.

Brigs popped out from behind the bar. "Yeah?"

"Call McGee and get him and a SWAT team over to the rest house on Edgewood Drive. Now! Tell them to expect trouble."

"Yes, sir!" Brigs answered and disappeared into the back.

Daniel pulled Alex out of building and shoved him into the passenger seat of a truck. "You are going to explain everything that's happened in the last two days," he demanded before slamming the door.

Alex nodded his head and tried to focus on the past two days' events, but the thought of Terra being in danger drove his dragon into a fit. He had to get there to make sure she was okay.

THE SOUNDS of a door opening pulled Terra from her nap. She moaned in pain as she tried not to wake up. Her head spun, and her stomach didn't like the motion. Swallowing hard, she tried to bury her pounding head into the pillow.

"He's not here," a male voice called.

Terra froze. She recognized that voice.

"But *she* is," another voice answered.

Oh God! Terra turned just in time to see a man in black closing on her. It was the same man who had knocked on her front door the day before. *Parker!* In this outfit, he looked like the mercenary she suspected him to be. Letting out a scream, she scrambled back across the bed.

Parker laughed and pounced on her. "Go ahead and fight," he said with a smile. "Makes my job more fun."

Struggling with all her might, Terra tried to get away, but he was larger than she was. It didn't take him long to have her pinned to the bed.

"Bring me a rope," Parker called out.

Brett stepped in with a length of rope in his scruffy hands.

Crying out, Terra fought as the men bound her hands and feet. After a few minutes of her screaming, they ripped a section out of the sheet and tied it around her mouth. She looked on, helpless, as they tossed the house, looking for something. They left nothing untouched.

"It's not here," Brett said as he dumped the dishes out of the cabinet to shatter on the floor. "What do we do?"

Parker paused and looked around at the chaos they had caused. He picked up Terra's cell phone and the note that had been dumped on the floor. "He'll be back," he said as he read over the note. "And we can use her for leverage." He held up the note for Brett to see.

An evil smile crept over Brett's face as he read the short message. "Right." There was a glee in his voice that sent a shiver of panic down Terra's spine.

Clicking into her phone, Parker sent a short text message before shoving it in his pocket. "That should get his attention." He turned to Brett. "Grab the girl."

Fear sent Terra squirming against her bonds again. There was no way they were going to take her without a fight.

Reaching out, Brett grabbed for her shoulders.

Terra twisted away from him.

"Come here, bitch," Brett growled as he placed one knee on the bed so he could get a hold on her.

Seeing an opening, Terra swung both legs up and nailed him in the side as hard as she could. The impact knocked him off balance but didn't do any real damage.

Brett growled in anger and pounced on Terra, pinning her shoulders to the bed.

She squirmed under the larger man, taking every opportunity she could to drive an elbow or knee into him. Lights danced behind her eyes as he punched her in the side of the head, but she still fought him. She would be damned if she went quietly.

"Stop." Parker's voice broke into their fight.

Brett dropped his body down over Terra's, pinning her to the mattress.

Squirming, Terra rolled her head over to look at Parker. She did not like the look on his face.

"Get off her," he said. "I have a better idea."

Slowly, Brett started to move.

Terra took the opportunity and swung her head back and straight into his face.

"Shit!" the man cursed and rolled off her.

An evil smile slipped across Terra's as he hit the floor with a bang.

"Fucking bitch!" he cursed again as he sat up. Blood ran down his face from where Terra's head had met with his nose.

Standing up, Brett raised his fist to lay another blow to Terra, but Parker grabbed his arm before the fist could fly.

"Wait," he said. "We still have that stuff the boss gave us."

Joy filled Brett's eyes. "Yeah." He looked over his shoulder at his partner. "That shit could kill her."

"And it would be painful."

Fear raced through Terra as Brett turned to look at her. He rubbed the back of his hand through the blood dripping from his nose, smearing it across his face. "Right…" Brett nodded and stepped out of the house.

Terra wiggled, trying to loosen her bonds. The fight had given her some slack, but not enough to make any real difference.

"It's all right, there, chicky." Parker came over and laid his large hand on Terra's cheek. "Look on the bright side—if you live, you'll have more power than you've ever dreamed of. But, of course, no one's lived through this yet."

Terra tried to jerk out from under his hand, but he pressed her head down into the bedding, holding her in place.

Parker laughed at her. "Just be a good little bird, and take your medicine." He stood up away from her to let Brett in.

"This might hurt... a lot," Brett said as he held out a hypodermic needle.

Terra lashed out, trying to hurt him again, but he was out of reach this time.

Aiming for her butt, Brett speared her with the needle. The force at which he threw it jabbed the needle through her thin clothing and deep into her muscle. A quick push of the plunger, and the liquid was in her.

"All done." He said it like she should be proud of him.

Terra glared at them both as the serum burnt its way through her. This one was worse than the last time she had been drugged. She whimpered in pain as it began to take effect. Closing her eyes, she tried to breathe through the aching, but it was too much. Her muscles tightened as the pain spread. Unable to take any more, Terra cried out in agony through the gag as she thrashed. Opening her eyes, she shot her attackers a death glare. Once she was free of these bonds, she was going to share this pain with both of them. That is, if she lived through it.

THE PHONE in Alex's bag pinged, and he nearly tore the flap off getting into it.

A message from Terra.

His relief turned to horror as he read the text. "They have her." His voice revealed the fear eating him. After all this time of looking, he had finally found a mate that his dragon wanted, and he had left her unprotected. "I have to go." Alex reached up and started to pull his shirt off. He could shift to his smaller size and fly out without Daniel having to stop.

"Wait!" Daniel reached out and grabbed his arm. "The men are on their way. Just stay put, and we'll be there shortly."

"But they said they would kill her if I didn't bring them the medallion." Alex squirmed in Daniel's grip. "I have to go."

"And they will kill you both if you give them that thing."

Alex let out a sigh and settled back into his seat. He'd told Daniel about the necklace and his suspicions. The fact that they had found Terra at the rest house just proved they had a spy in their midst. But who could it be? Obviously, it wasn't Daniel. He had been with Alex the entire time. They'd told Brigs to call the team and given them the location of the rest house, but it would've taken time to get someone out there. Even if they had called the men from his home, it would have taken longer to get there than the ten or so minutes since they had left the bar. No, these people had to have already known where he and Terra had gone. The only answer was the security system alerting the main office. "Who gets notified when one of the houses is used?" Alex looked up to Daniel, waiting for an answer.

"A few of the team heads and the on-call operator," Daniel answered quietly. It was clear from his expression that he was coming to the same conclusion as Alex. "There will be a full inquiry when this is over."

Anger flared into life in Alex. An *inquiry*? They could be killing his mate as they spoke, and Daniel's answer was an *inquiry*. "She's my *mate!*" Alex exploded. His hands flapped around as he tried to get Daniel to see his concern. "I *need* to go!"

Daniel glanced over at him. His jaw was set, but he drew in a deep breath and shook his head. "Then go, but the necklace stays here."

Nodding, Alex pulled off his clothing and shifted into his lesser form.

Rolling down the window, Daniel slowed so Alex could get out.

It was a tight squeeze, but Alex shoved himself out of the window and was on wing before he could hit the ground. He glanced back as Daniel stepped on the accelerator and hurtled the pickup down the road.

Tuning his mind to his task, Alex raced up and over the tops of the trees. He might get there faster if he stopped and shifted to his grand form, but that would take time—time his dragon would not allow him. He would just have to push himself as hard as he could and pray that it was enough.

HE SHOULD HAVE TAKEN the time and switched to his larger form. He had made the trip in his small form, but he had pushed himself harder than he had ever done before. His wings ached, and his breath came in ragged pants that ended in small puffs of smoke, but the end of his journey was in sight. He topped the trees surrounding the clearing and screeched out a roar that echoed across the field. There was a white sedan parked on the grass outside the cabin. Two men were manhandling Terra towards the open trunk. *Two targets. A heavyset black guy and a scrawny, white guy.* Alex picked the smaller of the two and rocketed straight for the man's face.

Screaming in terror, the man batted at the ball of hell that had been unleashed in his face.

Alex snapped and bit at anything he could get his teeth near as he raked the man's front with his claws. They went down in a heap of scales and flailing arms. Alex would have roasted the man if he hadn't fallen so close to where Terra had collapsed.

"Stop it, or she's dead!" the second man yelled.

Alex gave his victim one last chomp before turning to glare at the man holding Terra up by the head.

"Get off him, or I will break her neck right now!" he threatened, turning her head sharply to the side.

With a quiver of wings, Alex backed up until he stood on the ground on the other side of the downed man.

"Brett?" the man holding Terra called.

Alex glanced down at the fallen man. He wasn't about to get up. Ever. A few of those bites had hit the man in the throat, and he was pretty sure at least one had crushed something important. Licking the blood from his muzzle, Alex turned his attention back up to the man holding Terra hostage. Now, if Alex could just get a clean shot at him, he would be the next man down.

"Shit," the man cursed when he realized his friend wasn't going to get back up. He turned his attention to Alex. "Where's the necklace?"

So, they were *after the necklace.* "I don't have it!" Alex growled at him. His tail swished back and forth in agitation. Just let the guy loosen his grip on Terra—only one moment would give him the chance he needed to spring.

"Shift!" the man yelled at him.

Alex quivered in anticipation, waiting for the moment to strike.

"Shift, or she dies!"

Growling deep in his chest, Alex shifted back to his human form. He glared up from the ground where he was kneeling. "I don't have it." He lifted his hand up and scrubbed the back of it across his mouth, wiping the blood from his face.

The man's eyes widened in what Alex suspected was fear. "Where is it?" The man squeezed Terra's throat, making her face go red.

"It's in my bag," Alex growled. "I left it at The Dragon's Wing when I got your message."

This was obviously not the answer the man had wanted. The look that crossed his face was pained.

They both held their positions, waiting for the other to move. The man's hand on Terra's throat was the only thing keeping Alex from killing her attacker. A twitch from Terra's body drew Alex's attention down.

The man took advantage of the momentary lack of attention and threw Terra at Alex.

Alex scrambled to catch her as the man turned and ran to the car. All thought of chasing him left Alex's mind when that twitch turned into a spasm. He held her as she started to convulse. Forcing the side of his hand into her clenched teeth, he held her as a seizure racked her body. Had her attacker cut off the blood long enough to injure her? Or was this a side effect of the pheromones they had pumped into her system?

Clutching her to him, he protected Terra from the grass and dirt the car's tires slung out as her attacker escaped. Alex looked up and committed the plates to memory. He would hunt that man down and kill him as soon as he was sure Terra was okay. *No one hurts* Mine! *and gets away with it!*

The pain from Terra's clenched teeth eased, pulling his attention back down to the woman in his arms. The seizure was subsiding. He pulled his hand from her mouth and wiped the foam and blood away. With shaky fingers, Alex searched for a pulse in the side of her neck. It was there, but it was faster than it should have been. He pulled her farther into his lap as she started to shiver. Where the hell were Daniel and the SWAT team? He needed a medic here *now*!

The sound of squealing tires and crunching metal made Alex look down the road. The car was out of sight, but something had definitely happened to it. The sounds of gunfire rang through the woods. *Two. Three. Five. Someone was getting serious out there.* There were only a few people he could think of who would have a firefight out in the middle of these woods. Alex debated with himself. He should probably go and see who'd won, but that would mean he would have to put Terra down.

Mine! His instincts would not allow him to leave her unprotected again.

The seconds ticked by as he watched the road leading into the clearing. Movement drove a growl from him, and he pulled Terra closer to his body. No one was going to hurt his mate again. *Mine!* After a few seconds, he recognized Daniel coming towards him. Alex relaxed his grip, but only marginally.

Daniel held his shoulder as he jogged towards them. His shirtsleeve was soaked with blood. "Alex?" he called as he got closer. "Is she okay?"

Alex shook his head as he sat in the grass holding her.

Daniel's eyes ran over them both. "Is any of that blood hers?"

"No," Alex answered. His hands moved over her back, spreading more of the drying blood on her clothing.

Daniel glanced at the dead man sprawled on the grass. "Is any of it yours?" he asked.

Alex shook his head again. "No."

Nodding, Daniel turned and went to the house. He punched a few buttons on the security panel before turning back to Alex. "An ambulance is on the way."

Alex nodded but didn't look up. He was worried about how still Terra was in his arms. What if that seizure had caused some type of brain damage? He rolled her so she was facing up. She was completely limp in his arms. Carefully, he lifted her eyelid so he could check her. Her eyes responded to the light, but instead of the pupils being round, they were slitted like a cat's. *Or a dragon's.* Alex looked up at Daniel. He was staring down at them.

"We will figure this out," Daniel promised.

Turning away from his friend, Alex let Terra's eyelid go and held her to him. *What had those monsters done to her?*

Chapter 13

Someone was going to pay dearly for this as soon as he found out who was responsible. Alex sat in a well-worn hospital chair. Clutched in his fingers, he held Terra's limp hand. A machine near her head marked every beat of her heart, while a thin plastic tube dripped fluids into her veins. Three days he had sat there without food or sleep, waiting for some change in her condition, painfully aware of everyone who came into the room to check on her. Waiting for something to give him hope that she would be okay.

For three days, Alex had traced the patterns that shouldn't have been on her skin. Dragon scales. Not fully formed, hard scales like those that had covered him during his time in balance. These were soft scales, very much like those of a new baby dragon when they were first learning to shift. They pushed against the backside of her skin but couldn't quite make it through. *What the hell had those men given her?*

Alex let out an exhausted sigh and dropped his head

to the bed next to her, turned so that he could stare at their joined hands. The doctors were working on the drug they had found in the car Daniel had wrecked, but they were baffled. Yes, there were dragon hormones in it —both male and female. They were sure the large doses of hormones had caused Terra's seizure, but there was more in the mix than just those. There was a very fine powder they suspected was diamond dust, but they couldn't figure out why anyone would inject someone with diamond dust. The doctors had called in a mage to see if the dust was some form of magic spell. It held power, but nothing the mage had ever seen before. They were calling in a team to study it. But how long would that take?

Closing his eyes, Alex listened to the beeping of the machines. It gave out a steady rhythm that soothed his dragon. As long as that beeping was steady, *Mine!* was okay. His thumb rubbed across the rough skin as his tired mind worked on an answer to the problem. They would have had their answer had they captured either of the men from the attack, but both were dead—one by his hand, and the second by Daniel's.

If Daniel hadn't been so careless, they would have had their answer, Alex's dragon growled at him.

That's wrong. Daniel hadn't been careless. The man had fired first, and Daniel had defended himself. Had someone actually captured the man, Alex would have probably torn him to shreds after seeing what they had done to Terra.

The sound of the door opening pulled Alex from his thoughts. He lifted his head to see who had come to visit. His dragon ruffled his wings, ready to defend his mate if need be.

A single man walked in, carrying a paper sack and a backpack.

The ghost of a smile crept across Alex's face as he identified the familiar man. But, with his silvery hair, everyone in Eternity knew who he was.

"Hello, Michael." Alex's eyes traced over his friend. Michael looked just the same as the last time they had met, with the exception of his hair. There was one thin lock of gold flowing back from his temple —a mark from his bonding to Carissa. "How are you?"

Michael stopped and considered Alex. "Not bad." He gave Alex a warm smile to ease his next words. "You look like hell, though."

Alex just made a confirming noise in his throat. He probably did look like hell. Glancing down, he considered the scrubs the EMTs had forced him into when he'd refused to leave Terra's side. They were rumpled from the days he had spent huddled in that uncomfortable chair, waiting for some change in Terra's condition. There were traces of dried blood smeared on them because he hadn't taken the time away from Terra to wash properly. Yes, he was a mess.

Alex looked up as Michael came over and stood across the bed from him.

"How is she?" Michael asked as he stood over the bed, looking down at the sleeping woman.

Alex groaned as he shifted his stiff muscles and sat up. "Quiet," he answered, rubbing his thumb over the back of her hand. "She had a few fits when she first came in, but she's been calm ever since."

Michael nodded and looked down at her exposed arm. "And the scales?"

Alex glanced down at them. Those worried him. "They keep spreading."

In the few days she'd been there, the number of scales pushing at her skin had grown. They had started at her hand and had slowly been creeping up her arm. They were nearly to her shoulder now.

A worried noise rolled out of Michael's chest. "And she's not a dragon?"

"No, she's not."

They both waited in silence as they considered Terra's condition. Finally, Michael broke into the tension hanging in the air. "So how are you?"

A wry laugh slipped out of Alex in answer, but he didn't elaborate. If Michael couldn't already tell that he was an absolute wreck, then the man needed his head checked.

An amused grin turned the corner of Michael's mouth. "Have you eaten?"

Alex shook his head softly.

"Alex," Michael reprimanded him. "What good are you doing her if you don't take care of yourself?"

"I know," Alex said as he hunched over in his chair. "But..."

His dragon growled in frustration. Yes, he was hungry and needed food, but he couldn't leave his mate alone again. His bad decision to leave was what had put her in that bed in the first place. He looked up at

Michael, trying to find the right words to make the man understand.

Michael raised his hand, stopping any further explanation. "I know."

Of course he would know. Alex let out the breath he'd drawn in. For a moment, the fact that Michael was a bonded dragon had slipped his mind. He was so used to Michael being human. But he was dragon now. Michael would understand the need to protect what was his.

"Here." Michael reached out and dropped the paper sack on the bed in front of Alex. "When Daniel said you were here, I figured that you probably hadn't left to get food. Eat."

Alex let out a soft snort of amusement. "So Daniel knows I'm here?" He pulled the bag over and unrolled the top with one hand. The smell of hamburgers made his stomach protest its empty state.

"Of course Daniel knows you're here." Michael shook his head. "If you'd looked outside this room, you would've seen that he has a full security detail on this floor. And not just anyone..." He paused for emphasis. "The man's got SWAT out there."

This raised Alex's eyebrows in amazement. "SWAT?"

Michael nodded. Dropping his backpack on the floor, he leaned up against the wall and crossed his arms. "I'm not sure what's up, but once they got the bullet out of his shoulder, he ordered the SWAT team stationed on this floor and locked himself in his office. Carissa is beside herself, and the only time I've seen Kyle this mad was... well, when Carissa ran off with me."

Alex chuckled softly. "He *was* in a bit of a tiff that day." Pulling out one of the hamburgers, he peeled the paper back and looked up at Michael. "Do you want to know what's going on?" He took a bite out of the hamburger and nearly groaned in pleasure. That had been exactly what he'd needed.

"I think I can venture a guess."

Alex gave him a curious look as he devoured the rest of his burger.

"This has to do with the dead dragons."

Swallowing, Alex nodded his head. "Someone from Eternity is leaking information."

Shock stole over Michael's face. "We have a mole?"

Alex nodded as he pulled out the second burger and tore into it.

Michael turned his thoughts inwards. "I thought we'd solved that problem when we caught Jareth."

"Apparently not," Alex answered around the partially chewed burger in his mouth. He swallowed and went on. "There was a leak of information three days ago. It's how they found Terra."

"I knew something had gone down. Poor Reece has been put on administrative leave, but no one would say why," Michael said. "I guess he was on dispatch duty that day."

"I don't know, but when I find out who's responsible…" The rest of Alex's words trailed off in a threatening growl, and anger pounded at the back of his skull. As soon as he found out who had spilled their locations, they were going to be very dead. A note of regret slipped in. Hopefully, it was not Reece. The man had always been nice to Alex. It would be a shame to have to mangle him.

A snort of mirth came from Michael. "Well, you aren't going to do anything unless you take care of yourself," he pointed out. "When was the last time you slept?" He sniffed at the air. "Or showered?"

Alex glared at him.

"Look." Michael pushed away from the wall and picked up the backpack. "You're no good to her if you're exhausted." He set the bag on the foot of Terra's bed. "I stopped by The Dragon's Wing and picked up some of your stuff." Michael paused for a second, thinking. "Did you know someone trashed your locker?"

This brought a wry grin to Alex's face. "Yeah."

"Yeah." Michael echoed the irritated tone that had slipped into Alex's voice. "Brigs and I did our best to sort it out for you. Sorry, man. I couldn't just shove it all back in there like it was."

"Thanks." Although he hated when someone went through his things, Alex appreciated the gesture.

"Anyway," Michael continued, "what you need now is a nice hot shower and a nap."

"I'm not going to leave her," Alex protested. Hell would freeze over first.

"You don't have to." Michael pointed to the open bathroom door. "You can shower here, then either get dressed and go find a place to nap, or shift and curl up at the foot of her bed."

"But I can't leave her," Alex protested again. She needed him to protect her.

"Look," Michael said sternly. "You need rest."

"But—"

"And think about what she's going to say when she wakes up." Michael cut him off. "You reek. Do you think she is going to like that?"

Alex sat for a few minutes, thinking on his situation. He did reek. Badly. And he wasn't doing Terra any good, sitting there exhausted. Drawing in a deep breath, he let it out in a loud sigh. "But I can't leave her alone."

"Go wash. I'll stay here until you're done."

Looking up, Alex studied Michael's face. Michael had always been a solid and dependable guy. His transformation into a dragon hadn't changed that. Alex weighed his options. His dragon didn't like leaving her in the care of others, even if it was only to shower in the next room.

"You can even leave the door open," Michael offered, trying to coax him into agreeing.

Alex smiled. "All right." He was hesitant to let Terra out of his sight, but Michael did have a point. He wasn't doing her any good sitting there. Reluctantly, he turned loose of her hand. It was the first time he had released it since the doctors had settled her in that confounded bed. He patted it gently and stood up. "But just a quick shower."

Michael laughed as he stepped out of Alex's way. "I didn't expect anything more."

Shooting the man a glare, Alex picked up the backpack and went into the bathroom. A quick glance out the door gave him a great view of the head of the bed. A hint of a smile curled the corner of his mouth. He could get his shower without Terra being out of sight at all. Digging into the bag brought a full smile to Alex's lips. Michael had thought of everything. Clothing, soap, shaving equipment, a toothbrush, even a towel. Taking the things he would need, he stripped out of the scrubs and climbed into the shower stall. The temperature of the water made him jump when he turned it on, but it quickly warmed up.

Alex stood in the falling water and savored the feel. Even his dragon relaxed a little. This had been exactly what he had needed. Worry for Terra still ate at him, but the fresh water eased his tired mind. The best doctors in the area were working on her case. If Carissa Markel was worried enough to have Michael there, then the best mages were working on it, too. *They will find out what's wrong with her. She will be okay.* Alex kept repeating those two lines over and over as he washed and shaved. The inability to do anything for her was starting to drive him nuts.

A sound from the other room drew Alex's attention away from his thoughts.

"Alex!"

Tearing out of the shower, Alex raced into the hospital room, slinging water as he went. The sight that met him made his heart clench in fear. Michael had a knee up on the edge of the bed, trying to hold Terra down as she thrashed.

No! Shoving Michael out of the way, Alex caught Terra in his arms and pulled her up against him so she wouldn't hurt herself as she flailed. Immediately, her fit subsided. He sat on the edge of her bed, shocked, as she let out a soft moan and relaxed against him. *What the hell just happened?*

Turning his head, he looked down to where Michael lay sprawled on the floor. Surprise was plastered all over the fallen man's face.

Slowly, Michael pulled himself up from the floor. "What just happened?" he asked, verbalizing the question racing around Alex's head.

"I'm not sure," Alex confessed, "but I think you should go get the nurse."

Michael nodded and left to get the nurse on duty.

Bewildered, Alex turned his attention back the woman in his arms. When he'd come racing out of the bathroom, she'd appeared to be having another seizure, but that couldn't have been. No one calms down from a seizure that quickly. The look on her face was contented as he held her to his damp skin. He studied it for a moment. Something was different about her. Horror stole over him as he realized the change. The bones in her face had shifted, and fine scales had broken out over her skin. Holding his breath, he slid his hand down her back, praying it was normal. It was not.

Two long lumps stretched the skin along her back. *Wings.*

Chapter 14

"You're going to have to turn her loose," Carissa pleaded. "I can't look at her while you're wrapped around her like that."

Alex glared at her from where he lay in the hospital bed with Terra pressed against him. After Michael had come back with a nurse, Alex had forced himself to let her go so the nurse could check her over. He had just turned away to shut the water in the shower off and get a towel when Terra's fit resumed. After a few minutes, they discovered it was Alex's touch that held her to her current form. And that form was not pretty. The fit had pushed her further into a dragon form, but it wasn't a smooth transition. Rough patches of ugly, misshapen scales covered her body, while wickedly sharp talons tipped her fingers. Two half-formed wings poked out of her back. Her spine had lengthened, but she hadn't sprouted a tail yet. Alex had never seen anyone twisted as badly as Terra was. It looked painful, and that upset his dragon greatly.

"Come on," Kyle coaxed him. "Let us help."

Looking up at the king, Alex waffled for a moment before giving in. He could refuse them, but it would do him little good. The king had power over his dragon subject. Besides, they were there to help.

Reluctantly, Alex eased himself back from Terra. She moaned in distress as he climbed out of the bed. It took all of his willpower to not grab her back up against him. Turning his back to her, he closed his eyes. She let out another soft moan. His muscles tensed as he stood there, fighting the instinct to go help his mate. A body bumped into his side, and a hand landed on his opposite shoulder. Cracking open his eye, he glanced at the person holding him. Michael stood there, intensely watching the scene behind Alex as he gave Alex as much comfort as he could.

A strange sense of relief rolled through Alex. He had never been one to enjoy physical contact from anyone. Usually, it made his dragon cranky, but this... this comforted him. The simple touch gave him the strength he needed to stand there, helpless, as others tried to fix what was wrong with his mate. He shifted so his side was more solidly against Michael. The fingers at his shoulder tightened as the sounds of the scene behind him intensified.

"Kyle," Carissa's voice was heavy with concern, "she's caught between forms. Can you push her all the way to dragon?"

"I can try..."

Alex bit his lip, drawing blood, as he listened to the king attempt to force Terra into full dragon form.

Michael's hand clamped down harder when Terra moaned in pain. Alex shifted, trying to keep from turning around. His dragon was roaring to protect his mate, but he knew they were trying to help her.

"She won't go." The concern in Kyle's voice met Alex's ears.

Carissa made a worried noise. "Let me try."

The seconds ticked by at an agonizing rate as Alex listened to the king and his sister work to help Terra. He stood there with clenched fists, listening to his mate moan in pain as they tried to force her into a full shift. Magic tingled along his back as Carissa worked. Slowly, the sounds of Terra's distress subsided.

Did they fix her? The thought passed through Alex's mind, and he turned his head to glance back over his shoulder. Terra was back to her full human state. Michael's hand stayed on his shoulder as Alex turned around to face the bed.

A soft moan rose from Terra, and her eyelids fluttered open, then closed again.

Hope squeezed Alex's heart as he dropped to her side and took up her hand. "Terra?" he called to her.

Her eyes blinked a few times, unfocused, before finding him. There was confusion there, but she smiled as she recognized him.

Joy filled him as she squeezed his hand. *Mine!* was okay. Now, if they could just find a way to keep her that way.

OUCH. Terra wasn't sure what she had been doing, but every part of her hurt. A soft tingle ran along her nerves, driving the pain back to a dull ache. As the hurt subsided, her consciousness slowly returned. She tried to open her eyes, but the bright light of the white room drove a moan of pain from her, and she closed them again. Movement on her left drew her attention, and warmth enveloped her hand.

"Terra?"

She knew that voice. Slowly, her weary mind kicked in and gave it a name. *Alex*. Blinking to clear her vision, she turned towards the source of the warmth and sound. There he was, holding her hand. A warm smile crept across her face as she took him in. Something inside of her purred with delight that he was there. Her eyes traced over his kneeling form, and her smile widened. "You're naked again," she teased him weakly.

Joy flashed across his face, and he stood up to sit on the edge of her bed. His arms wrapped around her and pulled her in against his chest in a fierce hug. "Mine!" he whispered into her hair.

A contented rumble echoed up between them, surprising Terra. She pulled back from him, shocked at that sound. For a second, she thought the noise had come from him. It sounded like something he would make, but the vibration had rattled up from her own chest. She placed a hand over her sternum as the noise continued. *What the hell?*

Sympathy filled Alex's eyes as he reached out and caressed her face. "We will figure this out."

"Alex."

The soft sound of a woman's voice drew Terra's attention away from Alex and her new issue. Fear raced through her, and she clutched at Alex's arm. A beautiful woman stood next to the bed. Her golden hair was pulled up and held in place by a pair of bronze sticks. The woman's long dress was casual, but there was an elegant air to her that told Terra she was someone important. A man dressed in a button-down shirt stood behind her. He was taller but had the same golden hair and elegant air. Something about this pair pulled at the back of Terra's mind, but she just couldn't place them.

"Hello, Terra," the woman said with a gentle smile. "Just relax; we're here to help."

Some tension in Terra's chest unwound at the woman's calming voice, and the fear that had been racing through her eased as the woman went on.

"My name is Carissa, and this is my brother, Kyle." Carissa waved to the man behind her. "I know you've been through a lot, but we're going to help you figure it out."

At a loss for words, Terra glanced at Alex. Taking the nod he gave her as encouragement, Terra turned back to Carissa and asked the question she wanted to know the answer to. "What's going on?"

Carissa let out a long sigh and sat on the edge of the bed. "That's what we're trying to find out. How do you feel?"

How do I feel? Terra pondered that question for a moment. Up until Carissa had asked it, Terra had felt fine. A little tired, maybe, but now, not so much. The more she thought about it, the more it felt like something was moving under her skin.

"Weird," she answered, unable to explain the sensation. Something brushed against her mind, making her gasp. She dropped her head to her hand as a wave of fright and pain rolled through her, making her head spin.

Alex clutched her against his chest, and the sensation changed. The pain was still there, but need chased out the fright, and she clung to Alex as if her life depended on it. She needed Alex, but not in a physical way. Her soul needed him. This new sensation brought the fear and confusion back, and her hold on Alex tightened.

"Relax," the man Carissa had introduced as Kyle said soothingly. "He's not going anywhere." He brushed his hand down Terra's shoulder, and some of the tension and fear eased again.

A soft vibration rumbled up from Alex's chest. "I will never leave you again," he purred.

"But you will have to turn her loose," Carissa said. "We can't help her with you there."

Alex growled.

Terra smiled at the possessive tone of the noise. It made whatever curled inside of her happy.

"Alexander," the tone Kyle took with him held a stern warning.

Another angry growl rumbled out of Alex, but he reluctantly released Terra.

No! the thing curled up in her chest protested, *don't leave me!* A whimper slipped out before Terra could stop it.

"I'll be right here," Alex promised as he laid a kiss on the side of her head and stood up away from her. He squeezed her hand for a second longer before dropping it to the bed.

Terra wanted to say that it was fine, she didn't need him to hold her, but the thing curled up inside of her had other ideas. It roared in distress. The sound came out of her, scaring her. Pain raced along her nerve endings as heat burned through her. An anguished cry slipped out as something pushed against her skin, trying to force its way out. Immediately, hands were on her, holding her down. The burning and pain subsided, leaving her gasping for breath. Her skin hurt, and tears blurred her vision. She blinked them away, but something was wrong with her vision. The world was too sharp, and the colors were off.

"Terra?" Alex's soft voice called to her.

Turning her head, she looked at him. Her vision was still funky, but she could see the worry on his face. That thing inside her squirmed with the desire to comfort him. White-hot pain shot through her, making her scream again. Closing her eyes, she leaned her head back against the pillow and gasped for air. A soft thump on her bed drew her attention, and she cracked an eye to see what was going on.

A man with white hair stood next to Alex, waving his arms around as if he were talking, but no sound came out.

"Of course," Carissa answered the silent man.

Terra turned her attention to the woman.

"Michael is right," Carissa said as she stood up,

releasing her hold on Terra. "We're going about this the wrong way." She held her hand down for Terra to take. "By now, I should be used to dealing with a newly transformed dragon." Carissa shot Michael a warm smile before turning back to Terra. "Shall we try this again?"

Dragon? The thought bounced around Terra's head as she looked at the woman. She wanted to ask what she meant, but words were eluding her. Something was wrong, but she just couldn't understand it. Slowly, Terra placed her hand in Carissa's.

Carissa pulled her into a sitting position. She looked across the bed at Alex. "Hold her."

It took no time for Alex to find a seat on the bed behind Terra and pull her in against him. His arms wrapped protectively around her.

Whatever was inside Terra relaxed into Alex's warmth. She leaned back, savoring the feel of him against her skin. *Skin to skin.* Realization hit her, and she tensed in his arms. Her bare back was pressed into his bare front as the hospital gown she was wearing gaped open. It clung to one shoulder, but the snaps on the other side had been torn open in her struggles. She tried to shift away from him so she could fix her gown, but he wouldn't let her go. Slowly, she relaxed back into his hold as he cooed reassuring noises at her. The thing inside her wanted to be as close to him as possible.

A thing. That was the only way she could describe the ball of feelings bouncing around in her. It was need, desire, pain, and fear, all rolled into one terrifying package. And it was all separate from her own feelings, yet it controlled her body as much as she did.

The thing chirped at her, and she had an uncontrollable desire to snuggle into Alex. She pressed back against him as his arms tightened around her. Apparently, the thing felt safe there. The fear and tension drained from Terra, leaving her limp in his arms. Unable to draw up the energy to be afraid, she turned languid eyes towards Carissa. Her vision was still off, and it made the already gorgeous woman even more beautiful. A primal note of jealousy hit Terra, and she clenched her fingers into Alex's arms to keep him away from the other woman.

Alex shushed her softly and stroked his fingers over her skin, calming her.

Carissa studied the pair on the bed before sitting down on its edge. "Do you remember what happened?"

Terra's thoughts were slow in moving, but she could remember. "Two men came looking for Alex." Her words came out slurred as she spoke. There was a slight hiss to them. Terra stretched her jaw, trying to pop it. It felt like it wasn't in the right place.

"Yes," Carissa continued. "Do you remember them giving you an injection?"

There was no way she could forget the sting of that needle or the way the serum burned along her veins. "Yessss." There was that odd hiss again. Terra could feel Carissa's eyes run over her. The thing inside of her stirred for a second before calming down again.

"We think those men were trying to turn you into a dragon."

This time, when the thing brushed against her mind, it felt like the rough caress of scales under her skin.

Terra swallowed hard. How could they turn her into a dragon?

"How?"

Carissa let out a long sigh. "We're not sure, but you show all the classic signs of a dragon in distress." She paused for a moment before continuing. "Normally, it's a mental issue that can be addressed once we've forced the dragon into a single state, but that doesn't look to be the case here."

Terra considered her words. "What do you mean?"

"Well," Carissa began, "your form wants to go to dragon, but it can't get there." She glanced up at her brother before looking back at Terra. "Not even with our help."

Terra looked at her, confused.

"Somehow, your dragon is incomplete," Kyle explained. "It gets most of the way there, and then stops."

"But I'm not a dragon," Terra protested. She didn't know much about dragons, but she did know you had to be born a dragon. You couldn't make someone into a dragon. *Could you?*

Terra shivered as the thing inside of her moved. *Could that be a dragon?* It purred a positive note. Yes, whatever was inside of her was a dragon. *But it's not whole.* She didn't understand how she knew this, but she did. She looked up at Carissa. "Can you get it out?" The dragon in her roared in protest. The sound came out as a soft growl.

Carissa gave her an apologetic smile. "We aren't sure how they turned you into a dragon, so reversing the process is impossible." She took a long breath before continuing. "Other than the original myths, there's only been one case where a human has been turned into a dragon—" Carissa's eyes flipped up to the white-haired man for a moment. "—and that's Michael."

He smiled at her and mouthed something that made her smile in return.

Terra glanced between the two. *They're mates.* She paused as she tried to figure out how she knew that. The bit of dragon inside of her stretched itself. *It* knew. The fact that it had supplied her with the information surprised her.

"How?" she asked.

A wry smile crept across Carissa's face as she looked back down at Terra. "That's a long story. But that's not important right now. What *does* matter are you and your dragon."

Terra waited as Carissa paused, trying to gather her thoughts.

"I've been reading through the old texts, and I think there might be a way to fix what's wrong."

Hope radiated through Terra. Now that she knew what was curled up inside of her, she could separate it from her own feelings. The poor thing was confused and scared. That made Terra's heart ache. "How?"

"Someone will have to share a part of their dragon with you," Carissa said very carefully.

Alex's arms tightened around Terra, squishing her against her chest. "How?" he asked.

Carissa looked up at him. "She already has part of a dragon's essence in her. It shouldn't take much to complete what's already there. A scale from a bonded mate should do the trick."

Terra felt Alex draw in a deep breath as he considered Carissa's words.

"Use mine." The answer rumbled out of him.

A strange sense of contentment rolled through Terra at his words. Even as messed up as she was, he wanted her.

He's only doing it because he got you into this mess. The nagging thought popped into her brain. Terra wasn't sure if it came from her psyche or the damaged dragon, but it did have a point. Was he doing this out of duty? Or was there more there?

"I think we should leave that choice up to her." Carissa turned her attention back to Terra. "Do you understand what it means to be a bonded mate?"

A bonded mate? Terra thought about that for a moment. Alex had explained that dragons mated for life, but they hadn't had much time to talk about what it really meant.

"No," she answered. She needed to know what was asked of her before agreeing to something that was permanent.

Carissa gave Alex a surprised look.

He gave her back a shrug. "We haven't had much time to talk about it."

A wry smile slipped across Carissa's face. "I suspect you haven't." Drawing in another long breath, Carissa let it out slowly and focused on Terra.

Terra held her breath as she waited for the woman to go on.

"Well, to start, male dragons mate for life."

This Terra remembered from her talk with Alex, but something caught her attention. "*Male* dragons?"

Carissa nodded. "Only male dragons are driven to mate for life. Once they find a mate, they will devote the rest of their life to making her happy. On the other hand, female dragons are not driven to take a permanent mate. Females are driven to take the best male for their future brood." A smile spread across her face. "Knowing that their female may find a better mate makes most male dragons very fussy over their chosen mates."

Terra thought about that for a second. "But wouldn't that cause problems?"

Kyle let out a bark of laughter, but it didn't hold any joy in it.

"Yes," Carissa nodded her head. "It's been known to cause a few issues."

"Bloody wars," Kyle muttered angrily.

Carissa shot her brother a piercing glance. "But that was a long time ago." She turned her attention back to Terra. "Back when the survival of the species depended on who had the strongest blood. Nowadays, dragons tend to stick with their chosen mates by bonding."

"Bonding?" Terra asked.

"It's when a dragon gives a piece of themselves to their mate," Carissa explained. "It's a complicated process, but it's usually done by sharing a scale. I can tell you, it's not a very pleasant experience, but it joins the two mates together for life. It also allows a human mate to share some of the powers of their dragon mate. Like their longevity."

That made sense! That's why Alex's dragon had seen her as a potential mate despite her being human. Terra glanced over her shoulder to the man holding her. He had offered up his scale to help fix her condition, but that would leave them as a bonded pair, together until death. Was he doing it because that was what he wanted? Or was he offering himself as penance for leaving her unprotected? Terra focused back on Carissa. "And what if I refuse?"

Alex drew in a sharp breath and squeezed her tighter.

Carissa raised an eyebrow at Terra. "Besides shattering the heart of the man who's spent the last three days by your side?" She shrugged. "You would remain as you are—broken until we could find a way to either remove the dragon or heal it." An amused grin crept across her face. "At least you would have company in your stay."

Terra peeked over her shoulder at Alex. He had a grim-but-determined expression on his face. Yes, no matter what her answer was, he would stay with her. Warmth washed through her. The dragon inside of her liked the idea of being bonded with Alex. She closed her eyes and relaxed in his arms to think. Before everything had gone to pot, he had been interested in her as a mate. So much so that he'd been fighting with his dragon. She drew in a deep breath as she made her decision. It didn't matter what reason he had for offering himself up, his dragon had chosen her well before things had gone bad. She opened her eyes and grinned at Carissa.

"I'm already scared; I might as well be Terra Fied."

"Terrified?" Carissa asked, alarmed.

Terra laughed softly. "I'll take the scale." She paused and looked back at Alex. "That is, if you'll have me."

"Yes," Alex answered without pause of thought. He dropped his face to her shoulder and purred out a word. "Mine!"

Carissa laughed. "Then let me find a knife."

Michael pulled a pearl handled switchblade from his pocket and held it out.

"Always the Boy Scout," Carissa teased as she took the knife.

Michael shrugged and stepped back away from the bed.

"Now," Carissa turned her attention back to the bed, "we need a scale."

Alex nodded. "Right."

Terra turned just in time to watch scales shimmer over him as he shifted to his lesser form. He had been amazing before, but now, with her vision still messed up, he was dazzling. His scales caught the light and threw it out in rainbow hues. Her breath caught as he circled around her to lie in her lap. His tail wrapped up around her other side and draped across her legs.

Carissa laughed at him. "You couldn't get rid of him if you wanted."

Alex rumbled his annoyance with the woman, but he turned a sparkling eye to Terra. "Pick whichever one you like."

Terra stared at him, awed. He had chirped and squeaked at her, but she'd understood what he'd said. *How?* The dragon curled inside of her answered with a soft purr. Terra looked up at Carissa but couldn't find the words to express what she was feeling.

"Pick a scale," Carissa prompted her.

Nodding, Terra turned her attention to the dragon in her lap. Running her fingers over his glittering hide, she looked for just the right one. She petted him, feeling the ridges in his scales. When her fingers ran over a larger scale on his shoulder, the dragon inside of her gurgled.

"This one." She touched the scale again.

Carissa looked at the scale. "Good choice."

Kyle made an agreeing noise and stepped back out of Carissa's way.

Walking around the end of the bed, Carissa came up to stand next to Terra. Her hand came down to rest on Alex's shoulder just above the scale Terra had chosen. "Now comes the hard part."

Using the tip of the knife, Carissa wiggled the blade under the edge of the scale. She chanted softly as she worked.

Alex hissed and kneaded the bed with his claws as Carissa cut the scale from his shoulder.

Carissa grimaced as she pulled the scale free, and blood gushed from the wound. "Sorry," she said as she tried to press on the wound. "I had to take more than normal."

"I got it," Terra said as she covered the hole in Alex's shoulder and applied pressure. Magic tingled across her skin as she brushed against Carissa and the loosened scale.

"Thanks," Carissa said as she pulled back, leaving Terra holding the wound. "Um, I'm sorry, but this is going to hurt."

Terra nodded and bit down, waiting for the bite of the knife. It hurt as it went in, but the sharp edge slipped through the skin over her shoulder blade with ease. A tingle of magic washed over her as Carissa slipped the scale into the open cut. It hurt a little bit, but that was nothing compared to the burn that raced through her system as the scale settled into place. Terra screamed and collapsed forwards onto Alex as her world shattered apart.

ALEX KNEADED the bed as the point of the knife slipped under his scale. *God, that hurt!* He had heard that the sharing of scales was a painful experience, but he never expected to feel it clear to his soul. But then again, he would give up a thousand scales for Terra. The fact that she nearly refused him tore at his heart. Alex breathed through the pain and thought about her reaction. She had asked the same question when he had told her to refuse him at the hotel. The ache in his heart eased. She wasn't refusing him; she was checking all of her options and their consequences before making an informed decision. A wise choice. That, Alex could respect. One needed to know all the options when making a choice that would change one's life forever.

Her play on words floated back to him, and he smiled inwardly. Carissa had totally missed the reference. Terrified. Terra Fied. Even faced with an unknown future, she took the time to stop and crack a joke. It showed she had an indomitable spirit—something she was going to need in the coming months as she learned a new way of life.

Blood gushed down his side as Carissa cut the scale free, but he didn't hear what she said. More had been pulled away from him than just flesh. He sat there, stunned by the loss, as Terra pressed her hand over his wound. Her firm touch pulled him away from the shock.

It's for her, his dragon rumbled with contentment.

The loss was nothing compared to what he was gaining in trade. He shifted his head so he could watch as Carissa attached his scale.

Pain raced across Terra's face. She let out an ear-shattering scream and collapsed against him.

"*Terra!*" he roared and tensed up, but he dared not move underneath her.

Carissa reached for her, but Michael was at her side, holding her back. He shook his head and pointed at Terra. Kyle froze on the other side of the bed, watching.

Alex focused his eye on Terra and watched as patches of multicolored scales raced across her skin, and her form twisted. He could actually hear her bones creak as she shifted. It was the slowest and most agonizing shift he had ever witnessed. When she was done, she leaned against him, unconscious, in the perfect form of a lesser dragon. And blue as a star sapphire.

Shifting under her, Alex reached around and nuzzled her side, but she didn't respond to him.

"She'll be all right."

Alex looked up at Michael. Apparently, the man had reclaimed his voice from Carissa.

Michael leaned over and carefully pulled the IV away from Terra's foreleg. Her body had pushed the plastic tube out as it had shifted, and the liquid was leaking all over the bed. "My first shift was just as bad," he admitted, "only I didn't have the good fortune of passing out halfway through it." Gently, he lifted her off Alex and laid her back on the bed.

Free from her weight, Alex moved around so he could see her. She was beautiful. Her scales glittered softly in the light, almost the exact same shade as his. Two small horns curved back from her head. She was nearly a perfect copy of him, only smaller. He nosed her softly, trying to get her to wake up.

Kyle ran his hand down Alex's back, drawing his attention away from her. "Just let her rest."

Michael chuckled softly as he pulled the blanket up over her. "She's going to need it," he said wryly. "That first shift is exhausting. But stay with her. If she's anything like me, she's going to need you when she wakes up."

"Thank you," Alex chirped. Even if Michael hadn't suggested he stay, he was not going to leave her side until he knew she was okay. Carefully, he found a spot right up against her side and lifted his wing over her. Drawing in a deep breath, he relaxed next to her. Waiting for some change in her condition had been tiring, but the last few hours had completely exhausted him. With Terra's form stable and tucked safely under his wing, he could finally catch that nap he so desperately needed.

DAMN, *it was hot in here.* Terra shifted in her sleep, trying to get more comfortable. She kicked at the covers, but they didn't shift as she wanted them to. Growling her frustration, she tried to roll onto her side. Her back hit something solid and stopped her from getting into a more comfortable position. She had always been a side sleeper, and lying on her stomach wasn't comfortable. Growling again, she wiggled, trying to reach her goal, but something tangled around her legs. Visions of the men that had attacked her flashed in her head, and she thrashed, desperate to get away from them.

"Terra!"

The chirp of Alex's voice broke into her fear, and she froze in her struggles. A tingle of magic washed over her scales, and the weight that was holding her down lifted.

"It's all right."

Gentle hands rubbed down her back, pulling the blanket away from her. Rolling back to her stomach, Terra opened her eyes. Sleep clogged her vision, and she raised her hand to rub it way. It was an odd stretch, but she finally got her hand up to her face.

Alex caught it before she could clear her eye. "Careful," he cautioned as he rubbed her hand. "Your claws are sharp, and you could hurt yourself if you aren't careful."

Claws? Terra blinked away the sleep and turned to look at the man lying on the bed next to her. Her vision was still funky, but he looked as handsome as she remembered him being. But, he was bigger than she remembered.

Mine, some part of her purred in satisfaction.

Shaking her head, Terra tried to sit up, but she didn't bend right. She managed to push up to her hands and feet, but her balance was off, and she toppled over on her side.

Alex caught her before she could fall off the bed. "Easy there," he soothed. His fingers ran down her side in a soft caress. "You're dragon now, so things are going to be a little different. I'll help you as much as I can, but you might want to take it slowly."

Terra considered his words as she lay there. *I'm dragon now.* That she could believe. She felt different. Warmer. A stray thought raised her tail up and thumped it on the bed. She had a tail now! Another thought rustled her wings. She had wings! She felt both strange and wonderful at the same time.

Rolling her head over, she stared at the man next to her. He stretched down the bed with his head propped on his hand, watching her with those gorgeous eyes. She loved his eyes. And with her new vision, the colors in his hazel eyes sparkled.

All ours, that reptilian part of her purred.

Fear rubbed at the edge of Terra's mind. It felt as if something had invaded her brain.

I am you, that piece said soothingly.

No, you're not, Terra argued back. She had never had any part of her talk back to her before.

That part laughed. *We are one and the same.*

Doubt crept into her mind. *What do we do now?* she asked.

Go on, her dragon answered.

Terra paused to think about that. *Go on? But how?*

Another snicker crept out of the wayward bit. *We both want the same thing.*

Terra studied the man next to her as she considered what her dragon had said. It was true; she did want him. In more than one way. And that, in itself, was disconcerting. She barely knew the man, but she couldn't stand the thought of losing him.

He will not leave us, her dragon reassured her.

But does he love us? she asked, worried.

The answer came back to her in a mix of emotions. Desire. Need. An overwhelming possessiveness. None of it was love as she had known it. It was something much stronger.

But he's human, and we are not, Terra complained.

Then change that.

How?

The answer came rushing into Terra, and she instinctively knew what to do. Closing her eyes, she let go of the part of her that was dragon. Magic tingled across her skin as the scales slipped away, leaving her in human form. She heard Alex draw in a sharp breath and opened her eyes to look at him. Surprise rode his face.

For the Memory of Dragons

"Beautiful." The words slipped from him in a soft whisper as he reached out and pushed a stray lock of hair from her face.

See, her dragon gurgled at her, bringing the ghost of a smile to her lips.

Curling her hands up under her head, she considered Alex. His fingers played along her cheek and shoulder, sending shivers of delight through her. After a few minutes of enjoying his touch, she let out a sigh.

"Now what?" she asked, unsure of how to proceed. Everything about this situation was new and confusing. Not to mention, scary as hell.

Alex let out a soft laugh as he reached out and drew her in against him. "Whatever you like." He laid a kiss on her forehead. "We can take this as fast or as slow as you want."

Terra curled in his arms, thinking about that. *Whatever she liked*. She drew in a deep breath, filling her lungs with his scent. It was clean and rich, with a hint of spice and musk. Desire pooled in her core, and she knew where she wanted to start.

"Anything?" She pressed herself against him.

He laughed, and as he slid his hand down her back, he pulled her harder against him. "Anything," he purred as he leaned in and captured her lips for a kiss.

She savored his kiss as the passion built between them.

When he pulled back, the color of his eyes had darkened, and the evidence of his arousal was pressed firmly between them. "What does my lady desire?" There was a suggestive tone to his voice.

Terra bit her lip and looked up at him hopefully. "A big, fat, juicy steak. And a baked potato," she answered as her stomach rumbled.

Surprise flashed on his face from the unexpected answer, but he smiled. "As you wish." He kissed her quickly and went to roll out of the bed.

Catching him by the shoulder, she stopped him from getting up. It made her happy that he would give in to her demands even though he clearly wanted something else.

Alex looked at her, confused.

She smiled at him. "That is, as soon as we finish what we started back in that hotel room."

Letting out a growl born in desire, he pounced on her, reclaiming her lips.

Terra let out a giggle before letting herself be swept away in his passion. This whole dragon thing was going to take some getting used to, but as long as she had Alex there to help her, she could face anything.

Chapter 15

Daniel sat at his desk and looked over the stack of files spread out before him. He had triple-checked each file, trying to figure out who could have leaked the information about either the solitary dragons list or Alex's use of the rest house. Hours he had spent, checking phone records and alibis, trying to come up with some answer. Hours he had wasted. Everyone he had checked had been airtight. *How had the information slipped out without anyone knowing?*

Letting out a deep sigh, Daniel gathered up the files and slid them neatly into the box next to his desk. He would keep these files and watch these agents. Someone was going to slip up sooner or later, and he would be there to catch them. Now, he just had to worry about what to do until then. There were still a lot of people on the solitary dragons list that needed to be notified and relocated, just in case that was the common link. But who should he trust to do it? Only his finest agents had access to the entire list, and Alex was right. The dragons who had come up missing had been on all parts of the list.

How could any agent in Eternity give up dragons to be murdered? That thought ate at him. Their entire sworn duty was to protect dragons. These men had trained hard to achieve the status and rank they had, and for one of them to betray the very people they were sworn to protect was unthinkable. *Or more.* Daniel growled in anger. One of his men had already proven to be an agent for the group killing dragons, but he wasn't being any help to them. Somehow, even under lock and key, the man had found a way to take his own life before Daniel could get the chance to beat the information out of him.

Hell, they didn't even know who this group was. The only information they had was Alex's sketchy memory, the medallion he had recovered, two dead men, a few burner phones, and a car. Of all of that, the car proved to be the most useful. It contained several vials of some serum—the stuff they had injected Alex's girl with. He had every one of his scientists and mages researching the stuff to find out what it was and how it had changed the girl into a dragon. The idea that they could use a drug to change a human into a dragon was preposterous, yet it had happened.

Daniel clenched his jaw as he thought of the consequences of that. *How much would people pay for the ability to become a dragon? A lot! Was that why dragons were disappearing? So that someone could use them to make this wonder drug? Holy hell!* If that were the case, things were going to go to hell as soon as this group figured out how to make it work properly. If they found out it had only taken a bonding to complete the transformation, then all hell was going to break loose.

Daniel shoved the rest of the stuff off his desk and got up. He needed to get down to medical and get Alex put on the disabled list as soon as possible. With the gap in his memory, no one would question Daniel's decision. Then, he had to get Alex and the girl out of there before word got around that she had recovered and could turn into a dragon. Kyle had brought that information back to Daniel this morning, so suppressing the fact shouldn't be too hard. Daniel had a few old friends that he could send them to stay with until they could find the leak and stop this group. The next question was… how?

With no real leads, Daniel didn't know where to start. *There's the medallion.* He paused as the thought passed through his brain. This group had been very insistent on getting that thing back. Right now, it was locked up in the hidden safe in his office, and he was the only person who knew it was there. Maybe he should let that information slip out and see who came to collect it. No. This group was covering their tracks pretty well; they wouldn't be foolish enough to try anything in his office.

Daniel shook the idea away. Right now, he had to get Alex and his new mate to safety before something happened to them. Then, he could think about how to catch their mole. And once he did, someone was going to pay dearly for betraying his trust.

Click here to continue reading, For the Heart of Dragons, book 3 in the Dragons of Eternity Series

Acknowledgments

Dragons. Be them Asian dragons with their long bodies or European dragons with their strong wings, they are beautiful. They have always been one of my favorite mythological creatures. So when Marya asked for dragon stories, I was happy to offer up my contributions with On the Accidental Wings of Dragons. But I never expected it to go any further than that. So I was surprised when Rebecca came back and asked if I could expand the single novel into a series.

I said yes, but honestly, I was at a loss as the where I could go with the story. I could have followed Michael and Carissa as they learned to live with each other, but I wasn't sure if there was enough plot line in just that to give me a good story. I didn't really want to write a novel based solely on their romance. Sure it would make a fun read, but I like a little more plot in my novels than the traditional guy-works-to-get-girl motif you see in most romance novels.

I had to step back and reread the story to find the loose thread, but it was there, dangling in my face the whole time. I hadn't even considered the unaddressed mystery left hanging in the story. To me it had been a convenient reason to chain poor Michael up, not a plot device to drive a whole series. But in that one idea, I found enough fodder to drive this story on in to several books. It's amazing what you can do with a little loose end.

And of course it takes more than a plot device to make a book. It takes people. I have plenty of those supporting me on my way. I would like to thank all those that helped me on my path: my mother for listening to me and helping to bounce ideas; my family and friends for being there for me and understanding as I pounded away at my keyboard; the ladies at Crimson Tree for believing in me; my blogger friends for supporting me (even the ones that don't do fantasy…Ethan); and last but certainly not least, all of you readers that have made it this far with me in this journey. Thank you all from the bottom of my heart!

Also by Julie Wetzel

THE KINDLING FLAMES SERIES

Book 1: Kindling Flames: Gathering Tinder

Book 2: Kindling Flames: Flying Sparks

Book 3: Kindling Flames: Smoke Rising

Book 4: Kindling Flames: Stolen Fire

Book 5 : Kindling Flames: Burning Nights

Book 6: Kindling Flames: Blazing Moon

Novella: Kindling Flames: Granting Wishes

Boxed Set: Kindling Flames Boxed Set #1

Boxed Set: Kindling Flames Boxed Set #2

DRAGON'S OF ETERNITY SERIES

Book 1: On the Accidental Wings of Dragons

Book 2: For the Memory of Dragons

Book 3: For the Heart of Dragons

Book 4: A Castle for Dragons

Book 5: For the Kingdom of Dragons

STAND ALONE

White Lies

About the Author

Originally from Ohio, Julie always dreamed of a job in science. Either shooting for the stars or delving into the mysteries of volcanoes. But, life never leads where you expect. In 2007, she moved to Mississippi to be with her significant other.

Now a mother of a hyperactive red headed boy, what time she's not chasing down dirty socks and unsticking toys from the ceiling is spent crafting worlds readers can get lost in. Julie is a self-proclaimed bibliophile and lover of big words. She likes hiking, frogs, interesting earrings, and a plethora of other fun things.

Subscribe to Julie Wetzel's newsletter to get news on her new titles, giveaways, events, and more!

Julie would love to hear from you!
www.juliewetzel.com
juliectp@gmail.com

Made in the USA
Columbia, SC
17 August 2023